CW00501139

THE O'MALLEY & SWIFT CRIME THRILLERS

Corn Dolls
Foxton Girls
We All Fall Down
The House of Secrets
The Uninvited Guest
Deadly Games
One Last Breath
Still Waters
Vanishing Act
Chill Pill

VANISHING ACT

Copyright © 2024 by K.T. Galloway

Published worldwide by A.W.E. Publishing.

This edition published in 2024

Copyright © 2024 by K.T. Galloway. The right of K.T. Galloway to be identified as the author of this work has been asserted in accordance with the Copyright, Design and Patents Act 1988.

All rights reserved. No part of this book may be reproduced in any form or by any electronic or mechanical means, including information storage and retrieval systems, without written permission from the author, except for the use of brief quotations in a book review.

All characters and events in this book are entirely fictional. Any references to historical events, real people, or real locales are used fictitiously. Other names, characters, places, and incidents are the product of the author's imagination, and any resemblance to actual events or locales or persons, living or dead, is entirely coincidental.

Cover design by Kate Smith

Edited by GS & LW

VANISHING ACT

AN O'MALLEY & SWIFT NOVEL
BOOK 9

K.T. GALLOWAY

In the world of magic, nothing disappears without a trace.

When the celebrated illusionist, Gabriel Mirage, is found dead in the midst of his own vanishing act, O'Malley and Swift are thrust into a realm where the truth is as elusive as the disappearing act itself.

As the duo peel back the layers of deception, a fierce rivalry between magicians comes to light, and a clandestine society within the community is discovered.

When Swift does a vanishing act of his own, it's a race against time for the rest of the team to unravel cryptic messages, decode ancient secrets, and navigate a world where reality and illusion blur.

But is this world secret enough to kill for? And will O'Malley and Swift find out just how far they're willing to go to keep it that way?

Because nothing is as it seems, and the search for answers may prove more dangerous than any magical illusion.

MAILING LIST

Thank you for reading VANISHING ACT
(O'Malley & Swift Book Nine)

**While you're here, why not sign-up to my readers'
club where you be the first to hear my news, enter
competitions, and read exclusive content:**

<u>Join KT Galloway's Reader Club</u>
at ktgallowaybooks.com

ONE

Keith Stuckley was at his best when he was lying. It was all a game, he knew that. He loved it. Pulling on his tuxedo, his red silk waistcoat, and top hat and stepping up on to the stage as though he owned it. Keith was in his element. Keith was no longer Keith.

Gabriel Mirage.

That's who people knew him as. The great and powerful Gabriel Mirage. Illusionist. Magician. Deity? He might not go quite that far, but his fans certainly did. Not only did they flock from miles around to see Gabriel Mirage in action, but they also flooded his post with letters and his inbox with mail, gushing about their love for him.

There was a part of him, shoved deep down, that knew Keith Stuckley wouldn't get that kind of treatment. His post was bills, bills, and more bills. But when he was in his top hat, no one could tell Gabriel

Mirage he was overdrawn, and his electricity was about to be switched off.

Gabriel Mirage made his own electricity.

Keith laughed at himself, sat down at his dressing table in the small flat above his theatre, and started on his show make-up, dabbing his face with foundation to hide the wrinkles that seemed to multiply nightly, concealer to lighten the dark smudges under his eyes deepened by money worries, then powder to set it all, and blusher so he looked alive under the stage lighting. He drew a thin moustache with an eyeliner pencil, because people expected him to look like the poster boy of old, and filled in his thinning brows. Finally, pouting at himself in the mirror, Keith felt the shift of power inside him. The bubbling confidence that came with transforming himself into someone new. Someone people loved.

Tonight's show was going to be a good one, he could feel it in the way the air shifted around him. It was his birthday tomorrow; forty. Keith dabbed a little extra concealer under his eyes. Even though he'd not quite made the millions he always said he would before he hit his fortieth birthday, Gabriel Mirage was world renowned, *and* he had his own venue. Not a lot of magicians could say that. Gabriel was no longer running the circuit, grabbing shows where he could and filling his down time with birthday parties. Gabriel had a stage he called his own. Keith owned the flat above it. That's how he split his two worlds.

A young boy ran into the room and grabbed at the

2

hairbrush on the dressing table, whacking Keith over the head with it.

"Dad, dad, I'm helping, I'm helping," the boy cried, excitedly.

Keith laughed, putting his hand over the boy's and guiding the brush a tad softer, sweeping it away from his face.

"Thank you, Benjy," Keith said, ruffling the boy's own hair with his free hand. "But shouldn't you be in bed?"

Benjy pouted, his blue eyes flashing in the dressing table lights. Keith took his son's hand and led him through the flat to his little bedroom. Settling him back down in the spaceship shaped bed and turning on the night light. It was a well-versed routine when it was Show Night. Benjy liked to watch from the wings, but Keith thought that at five he was a little too young to see his dad wrapped in chains and struggling to break free, or locked in a box and magically disappearing. Yet, there was no one else in the flat to make sure he didn't wander, and when Keith was Gabriel, he was in a world of his own.

It had been just the two of them for the last few years. Benjy's mum was gone, almost as though she'd been one of Gabriel's magic acts. In reality, though, Keith knew she wasn't that far away from the family she'd forgotten about because they weren't enough for her.

It's enough for me. We don't need her. Keith kissed Benjy on the top of his head, inhaling his achingly familiar scent. Soon he'd stop smelling like baby powder and sweets and the scent of pre-teen sweat would kick in. And then Keith probably wouldn't be allowed to get anywhere near his head to kiss it, given what Keith had been like himself as a twelve-year-old boy.

"Go to sleep while Daddy works, Benjyboo," Keith whispered, a cold shiver tickling his neck. "I'll come and say goodnight when the show's over. Love you, baby boy."

"Love you, Daddy," Benjy said, sleepily.

Keith kissed his son again, pulling the duvet up and tucking it around the young boy's chin so he didn't catch a cold. It may have been almost spring like now, but the April evenings still packed an icy punch.

The draft came again, wrapping itself around Keith's neck like a scarf, blowing up from the theatre itself. There was no reason for a draft with the doors and windows shut tight down there. Keith made sure that the theatre, at least, was warm. He couldn't have the cold keeping the punters away. He pulled up the collar of his dressing gown and hurried back across the hallway to his room, passing the stairs to the theatre as he went. Both stairwell doors were open; top and bottom. That was weird, Keith could have sworn he'd shut them. Glancing down into the muted light of the stairwell he saw a figure glide across the foot of the stairs. A lump of move-ment in the almost darkness. Keith's body tensed, his

4

skin prickling. Was there someone down there? Or some*thing*?

Come on, Keith. You're Gabriel now, not afraid of anything. Especially things that aren't real.

He puffed out a breath and looked again at the stairs, peering down into the gloom with a hammering heart. It was empty, just as he knew it would be. The panic was always the same on show night, heightening an anxiety that had grown in Keith like a cancer since he was left in sole charge of his son.

"Of course there's no-one there," he said aloud, the way his therapist had told him to.

Try to confront the fears, Keith, she'd said, as though the fears were somehow tangible objects he could capture and contain in the magic chest where he kept his ribbons and ropes.

He'd pretended he was okay after six sessions. Offering her tickets to his show as an extra thank you on top of the sixty pound an hour he couldn't afford. She'd still not been to see it.

Keith walked to his bedroom and closed the door behind him. A bolt of panic speared his chest as a draft tickled at his ankles.

"It's windy outside, Keith," he said, untying his robe and slipping deeper into the facade of Gabriel. The tuxedo was getting a little tight around the stomach, but if he breathed in for a moment, Keith could get the buttons done up enough to hold. "The wind is finding its way into the cracks in the old building."

There were rumours that the whole pier was

5

haunted. Keith's tiny theatre perched right at the tip was the site of an historic massacre of some sort or another. But when Keith bought the place twenty years ago, he'd done his own research, and the theatre was only built in the eighties. The pier just a few decades earlier. It was a new structure, built to rival Cromer or Great Yarmouth. But Wexwade was in the arse end of nowhere and rivalled nothing.

Maybe that's why the rumours started, Keith thought, reapplying his thin moustache and waxing down his dark hair. *Everyone loves a ghost story.*

And Wexwade Theatre was a ghoul-free business, well, apart from the famous Gabriel Mirage Halloween shows, and even those spectres were a light projector he'd got on sale from HomeBase. But recently, there had been times when Keith had felt the presence of another person near him. Heard bumps in the night that made no sense. It was all starting to take a toll.

With one final look in the mirror, newly transformed Gabriel pulled back his shoulders and readied himself. He'd already prepped the theatre, checked all his props were working and safe and tucked away in the wings of the stage. Now all that was left was to head back down there and open the doors. So why did it feel like he was about to embark on a mission to Mars and not something he did regularly?

The door at the foot of the stairs swung properly open on its hinges with a creak and a rush of freezing cold air. Shutting it behind him to keep Benjy safe, Gabriel moved backstage to the switchboard, flicking on the lights and illuminating the theatre. The bubble of panic spread across his chest and no amount of deep breathing would shift it. Stepping past the vanishing cabinet, Gabriel stroked the warm wood, checking again that the door to the cabinet was shut tight. A shuffle across stage right made the hairs on the back of his neck stand to attention and his throat constrict. The shadow from earlier. The movements in the darkness. Maybe it wasn't ghosts.

He pulled back the curtains and peered out onto the stage and the empty auditorium rising beyond it. There was no one there. Real or not real. But he could have sworn he'd heard someone. Gabriel pulled his head back and shook the curtains straight with the creeping awareness that someone was watching him. That he wasn't alone backstage. He turned his head, slowly, wanting to both see what was behind him and wanting to shut his eyes and run back up to his flat. He could feel it, a breath on his neck, warm and close and stale. Gabriel felt his stomach turning over, his heart hammering so hard in his chest it pitched him forwards with every beat.

Come on!

Forcing himself to turn, Gabriel felt his bladder loosen as he came face to face with a monster slithering out of the darkened corners. He tried to make sense of it. Giant, a hollow face, a... wait. With a stutter, Gabriel reached out an arm and whacked the monster around the head. It clattered to the floor, the top hat rolling around in circles until it came to a juddering halt. Not a monster at all, just a coat stand with a top hat and cloak.

You're losing it, Keith.

Gabriel picked up the hat and cloak and pulled them on, his hammering heart showing no signs of slowing. The noise had probably been the boards on the stage shifting under the warmth of the lights. Yes, that would be it.

Either that, or Candy, the local teen Gabriel hired to check tickets and patrol the auditorium to make sure everyone was okay during the show. Sometimes Candy let herself in on the days the front doors weren't locked. But Gabriel was sure he'd locked up earlier, after Benjy and he had come back from paddling in the sea. Maybe he'd forgotten, Benjy had been whinging about being hungry.

Whatever it had been, it was nothing to be scared of. Gabriel shook himself down and marched to the dimmerboard to lift the auditorium lights and dim the stage lights, pulling up the slider to cast the stage front in an eerie red glow. He loved listening to the oohs and ahhs of the audience as they made their way in and caught sight of the backdrop glittering in the lights and the swathes of red velvet curtains.

If he was quick, he could unbolt the door for Candy and be back here in time to see this evening's first arrivals. With a swish of his cape, Gabriel flew through the theatre to the front doors, determined that his birthday show would be one that the punters would talk about for years to come.

TWO

I<small>T WAS A DATE,</small> A<small>NNIE WAS PRETTY SURE OF IT.</small> I<small>F IT</small> wasn't a date, there'd be no reason for her hair to be sweating. Whose *hair* sweats? Armpits, yes. Backs of knees, yes. Hands, yes. But hair? Annie was glad she'd opted to tie it back because with the added moisture her normally large bouffant was triple sized and threatening to need its own ticket to the show.

She wiped her hands on her jeans and looked around for Swift. The foyer of the small theatre was filling up with families, couples, people on their own busy staring at their phones. Annie wondered if all the lone people were waiting for their dates too.

Dates, ha, it was comical to Annie that after almost three years of working together she was going on a date with her boss. Not least because he was her boss.

DI Joe Swift was in charge of a branch of the

Major Crime Unit at Norfolk Constabulary. He'd brought Annie on board to help with a case she was already embroiled in; she'd solved it, and the rest is history. Only it wasn't quite history, because Annie had never left the team and now loved getting her teeth into MCU cases, using her skills as a psychotherapist to catch the bad guys. From narcissistic schoolgirls to bubonic plague to spa hotels crumbling into the sea, there was never a dull day in the MCU team.

DS Belle 'Tink' Lock and DC Tom Page made up the rest of the team and they had been hinting at Annie for a while now that Swift had a soft spot for her. But Annie never let her hopes get raised, not until this evening.

The doors to the theatre clattered open and another round of people bustled in bringing the cold night with them. Annie glanced over, her heart thumping when she caught sight of the top of Swift's head over the crowd. She tuned out the chatter and made her way through the thick body of people.

"Excuse me," she uttered, squeezing between a woman with a buggy and a man with a comb over. "Pardon me."

The windows in the foyer were starting to fog, the air was getting thick with recycled breath. Annie ploughed on, shuffling through the bodies until she found herself face to face with Swift. With little room to manoeuvre, Annie was acutely aware that personal space wasn't something she was able to offer. She adjusted her neck so her face wasn't stuck in his chest and gave him a smile.

"Hi Joe," she squeaked.

"Annie," Swift replied, his face shiny. "How are you? Looking good."

Manipulating his back and neck into an origami shape, he leant and gave Annie a kiss on the cheek.

Only a few hours had passed since they had last seen each other, but right now Annie felt like a small child on the first day of school. In the office they'd been talking non-stop about the Lowanford Lake case they'd just closed. Annie had no trouble thinking in cohesive sentences about the parents who'd stopped at nothing to protect their child or the unsuspecting victims who'd been pawns in their experiments. It was easy at work, they had lots to talk about.

Currently, there was nothing but a dancing monkey in her brain, clapping its symbols together in a bid to make some noise. No matter how hard she tried, Annie could not think of one thing to say to Swift.

"Hot, isn't it?" she said eventually, cursing the dancing monkey.

Swift pulled at the collar of his t-shirt under his jacket, corroborating her point.

The foyer was filling up with yet more people, despite there being no room. Annie stood on her tip toes and searched the crowds for a clue as to the pile up. It was getting uncomfortably busy and if any more people decided to force their way into the theatre foyer, then Annie would be able to lift her feet off the floor and stay upright.

"Coming through," a voice shouted behind her. "Out the way. Mind your backs."

A young girl, still in her teens, was elbowing her way through the foyer. With a steely look on her face, she pushed past people twice her size to make room.

"Stupid Keith and his stupid time keeping." Annie heard the girl mutter as she pushed past her and Swift, seemingly not worrying about the time as she stopped to double take a look at the DI. He got that a lot, DI Joe Swift, always a favourite with the ladies and some of the men too. Annie felt her stomach flutter at the thought she was on a date, though to be fair, it could have been someone's elbow jabbing her.

Once the girl had reached her destination and unlocked the doors to the theatre itself, the room heaved a sigh of relief. The busy chatter faded as people started to take their seats and the foyer emptied until it was just Annie and Swift and a few stragglers left.

"Drink?" Swift asked, nodding to the tiny, unmanned bar.

"If you're going to offer to steal it for me then yes, please," Annie smiled.

"I'll leave an IOU," Swift said. "I'm parched."

It had been Swift's idea to come and see a magic show. Thinking outside the box, Annie had thought, but now she was wondering if he'd invited her here because it was in the middle of nowhere and there was less of a chance of bumping into someone they knew.

Swift handed her a can of Coke, condensation dripping down the side. It was deliciously refreshing in her hands, but she resisted the temptation to tuck it into her hair to cool down her sweaty scalp.

"I hope the show is less of an ordeal than the pre-show warm up," Swift said, his lips pulling into a grin. He cracked open his own drink and took a swig.

"Oy, thief. Spit that out right now or I'll have to report you to the police." The young girl swiped the can of Coke from Swift's hands so quickly she could have been auditioning for a part in Oliver!

The DI stumbled backwards, his hands up around his head to protect himself. Annie couldn't help but laugh at the sight. A six-foot something police officer taken down by a teenage waif.

"I am the police," he yelped from behind the crook of his elbow. "I left a fiver in the fridge for them."

The girl paled as she thrust the can back into Swift's hands, sugary liquid spilling out onto his fingers. "It's not my fault, don't arrest me. I'm on me own and Keith didn't even let me in the building. How am I supposed to check tickets and serve drinks and let everyone in the show if I can't get in the bloody door?"

It wasn't a question that needed an answer, which was good as the girl was already disappearing back into the auditorium, her words trailing behind her.

"Doesn't bode well," Annie said, looking at her can and wondering if it was safe to drink.

"Maybe it's all part of the act?" Swift leant against the counter. "The great and wonderful Gabriel Mirage is actually a panto in disguise?"

"Or a clown?" Annie laughed.

"Oh no you didn't," Swift said, beaming.

It was a good distraction; Annie hadn't thought about her sweaty scalp for a few seconds and she felt herself relax. It's just Swift, the guy she spends all day everyday with, the guy who put her up when she couldn't manage her own stairs with a broken ankle, the guy who made her laugh as much as he annoyed her, the guy who went up against an explosive device for her, the guy who flew to Spain to make sure she was okay. Annie glanced over at the DI; yep, it's just Swift.

And, it would seem, Tink and Page.

"Sorry we're late," Page said, bundling Tink through the door in front of him. "This one wouldn't be able to find a tree in a desert unless it had an arrow pointing to it."

"Excuse me." Tink bundled Page back but with his mountain of muscles he barely moved. "I could have left you to get the bus, which would have been hard given that Wexwade is so far in the middle of nowhere that there is no bus. So, maybe I could have left you to walk."

Tink gave Annie a hug before stealing a swig of Swift's drink.

"Evening," Swift said, nodding a welcome to the rest of the team. "Shall we take our seats?"

"If Tink can find it," said Page, giggling and ducking out the way of Tink's outstretched hand.

"After you," said Swift as he ushered his team into the auditorium.

Annie ducked her head and marched through the doors, feeling silly and glad she hadn't dressed up too much. She dug her hands in the pocket of her jeans and pulled out her ticket, eyeing the seat number.

"We were an afterthought," whispered Tink, linking her arm through Annie's. "Swift called me last night and asked if I'd bring along Page too. That took a bit more persuading, can you believe that oaf has a better social life that I do?"

"Right." Annie looked at Swift who was studying his ticket like it held the secret of life.

Tink squeezed Annie's arm and pulled her up the stairs to the back of the theatre and their seats. They had a small row to themselves. Tink and Annie shuffled to the side, followed by Page then Swift who bagsied the aisle seat so he could stretch out his long legs.

"Honestly," said Tink. "The doughnut said he'd invited you and then he was worried that you'd feel awkward without the rest of the team here. If he would have been in the same room as me I'd have knocked some sense into him, but that's hard to do over the phone. Baby steps, Annie. Baby steps."

Before Annie could reply that if Swift's baby steps got any smaller, they'd be going backwards, the lights dimmed, and a chorus of eerie music filled the air. The auditorium hushed, the music rose in a crescendo. Spotlights danced across the stage which was empty but for a large cabinet that could have worked as an ornate wardrobe. Annie had seen something like it before, a hazy memory from childhood of a trip with her mum and dad to a magic show in London. The magician back then had appeared and disappeared through the doors of the cabinet like, well, magic. Annie cherished those memories, the ones that came before her happy family all but disappeared itself.

As the cymbals crashed and the electronic piano rounded the top of its chords, a host of sparklers set off across the bottom of the stage. No matter what Annie had been expecting from this evening, she was determined to enjoy the show, and this was promising. At least, it would be if the magician had appeared before the crescendo petered out. Seconds passed, then minutes, the pre-recorded music was still playing but the stage was empty. A Mexican wave of chatter started to grow through the crowd, people turned their heads to look at each other and the doors and the stage again. Everyone was waiting for Gabriel Mirage to magic himself onto the stage.

"Maybe he's locked himself in," Tink whispered.

Seemingly, the young girl from earlier had the same idea, as she stepped out from the wings and scuttled across the stage.

"Keith, er I mean, Gabriel Mirage." Her voice carried across the stage and all the way up to the back row where a heavy feeling was settling in Annie's stomach. "Are you okay? Do you need some help?"

Annie bolted upright, panic spreading through her making her move.

"Something's wrong," she said to the rest of her team. "Let me past."

The seats were so closely packed that Annie had to climb over Page's legs to get past him. Swift was already on his feet, his brows knitted together.

"Gabriel," the girl said to the closed doors. "I'm coming in."

Annie and Swift looked at each other, their faces mirrored.

"No," they cried, running down the stairs towards the stage. "Don't open those doors."

But they were too late. The girl tugged at the doors, pulling them towards her. Something cracked inside the wood, thumping out onto the stage floor, and rolling to the feet of the young girl. She screamed; a bloodcurdling pitch that echoed off the theatre walls.

From the front of the stage, through the crackling sparklers and the dizzying movement of the spot-lights, Annie saw a monster. She tried to call to Swift, but she couldn't. The monster was facing her with bloodied holes where its eyes should have been. She pushed through the fear and jumped up onto the stage, gathering the still screaming girl in her arms.

"It's okay, it'll be okay," she said, trying to calm her down as Swift approached the body and shook his head.

But it wasn't going to be okay, not for Gabriel Mirage.

THREE

IT TOOK ALMOST FIFTEEN MINUTES FOR TINK AND Page to clear the auditorium. Whilst some of the crowd left as quickly as they could, others were here for a show and were darn well going to get one. Even if that show was a dead magician and his traumatised assistant.

Annie felt the rush of adrenaline starting to seep away; her teeth chattered, and her legs felt like jelly. She had led the young girl across the stage and out into the wings where they sat together on a couple of old boxes while Swift had set up a cordon around the body of Gabriel Mirage. They'd listened in stunned silence as Tink had called it in, and now they waited in limbo for the forensic team to arrive.

Tink dropped down on a box next to Annie and handed her a can of Tango.

"For the girl," she said, hauling herself up again

and pushing through a heavy curtain onto the stage to talk to Swift.

"Here, drink this, the sugar will help with the shock." Annie cracked open the can and handed it to the girl who took it with shaking hands. "Can you tell me your name?"

"Candy," the girl replied. "Candy Atherton. I live in the village and my mum has known Keith forever. Oh god, I need to tell my mum what's happened."

"All in good time, Candy," Annie said, softly. "We can do that for you, if you'd like us to. Is Keith Gabriel's real name?"

Candy nodded, clutching the can of drink close to her chest. Annie sat in silence, letting the girl drink and replenish her energy; she knew better than to start barraging her with questions this early on. There was only so far the human brain could be stretched, and Annie wasn't about to push it with Candy, whose brain couldn't be much older than seventeen.

The silence backstage was intimidating enough to give Annie goosebumps. Every miniscule sound was muffled by thick fabrics and boxes and the shape of the wings, designed to keep noise away from the stage, had the same effect behind the scenes too. She rubbed her arms and pulled her coat across her chest, ignoring the pungent smell that was tickling her nose.

"You get used to it," said Candy.

Annie looked at her quizzically.

"The chills back here," Candy went on. "It's said to

be haunted, but that's rubbish. Keith just doesn't like paying the bills, so the place is always bloody freezing. The only place he heats other than the auditorium is…"

Annie didn't think she'd seen anyone dissolve so quickly in front of her eyes before. Candy's face drained of colour, her bloodshot eyes widened with a look so petrified it made Annie's skin tighten and crawl across her bones.

"What?" asked Annie, glancing over her shoulder. "Candy what is it?"

Candy grabbed at Annie's wrist, her bony fingers stronger than Annie gave her credit for. "Benjy, oh god, poor Benjy. Someone needs to check he's okay. What if he snuck into the audience again tonight? He might have seen…"

Candy jumped up and ran towards a door at the back of the stage, pulling it open and disappearing through it. Annie followed quickly behind her and up a flight of stairs to a small apartment. The home was surprisingly warm and well decorated. Pictures hung on the dark green walls of the hallway, a man Annie recognised as Gabriel Mirage but in normal clothes and, weirdly, no moustache. There was a boy in a lot of the photos too and Annie felt her stomach flip; this must be Benjy. Annie followed the sound of Candy's voice to the far end of the corridor.

"Is Benjy Keith's son?" asked Annie, as Candy pushed open a door as quietly as possible.

The room glowed with a soft orange night-light, just enough for Annie to see the sleeping figure of a small boy. He was tucked into his bed, sweaty hair sticking up all over his pillow. A lump formed in her throat and she had to take a few grounding breaths before turning back to Candy and indicating they should leave.

"Is there a mum around?" Annie whispered, trying the next door along the corridor and ushering Candy inside.

The living room was as loved as the rest of the apartment seemed to be. Farrow and Ball grey walls enclosed squishy sofas and a jungle of plants. There was a small kitchenette attached to the living space and Annie moved to get a glass of water for them both.

"Keith hasn't spoken in a while about Benjy's mum," Candy said, taking her glass. "I think she's still alive, but it's always been the two of them as long as I've known them. Mum will know more. What will happen to him?"

"Any grandparents?" Annie asked, avoiding the question.

Candy looked wide eyed. "I don't know."

"Then we have a specialist team to help look after children in times like this. Try not to worry, Candy." Annie sipped her water, her mind a thick knot of unanswered questions. "Do you feel up to talking about this evening? I think we'll need to stay put now, so we don't contaminate any more of the crime scene, but the sooner we can work out who did this to Keith, the sooner we can get things sorted for Benjy."

Candy moved her glass around in her hands, condensation dripping down onto her fingers. Annie watched her study the water and draw patterns in the moisture before she looked up and nodded.

"Can you tell me how a normal show night pans out?"

Candy bit her bottom lip, chewing for a while before she spoke. "Keith does it all, mostly. He sets up his shows, he's a bit of a one-man band."

Annie nodded in encouragement, noticing the way Candy still spoke about Keith in the present tense.

"I just arrive to take tickets and man the bar, that kind of thing." Candy looked towards the door. "I'm also in charge of making sure Benjy doesn't walk onto the stage when the show is on. He sometimes likes to stay up and watch, but Keith doesn't like him seeing the gory stuff, you know?" She looked up at Annie, her eyes brimming with tears. "Who could have done something so horrible to Keith? He's one of the nicest people I know... knew."

"We're going to do our best to find out, Candy,' Annie said. "Can you tell me what happened this evening? When we were in the auditorium, I thought I heard you saying you'd been locked out, was that something that happened regularly?"

Candy shook her head. "Keith was never late. He always got the door open for me an hour before the show started. People like to arrive early and make sure they're in their seats for ages before the shows now, it's weird if you ask me. But anyway, this evening I arrived, and the theatre doors were still locked. There's no other way in. The fire escape doesn't open from the outside."

Annie made a mental note of that. "How *did* you get in?"

"I had to climb in the toilet window and unbolt the door that way." Candy looked at Annie, her brows crinkled. "You're not going to arrest me for breaking in, are you?"

Annie shook her head. "Absolutely not. This window, is it big enough for an adult to climb through?"

"I barely fit, so unless that adult is as small as me, then I'm guessing no."

Candy was a small teenager, five foot nothing with limbs like twigs. There was no way an adult would have been able to get into the theatre the same way Candy had done.

"What about after you were inside?" Annie went on. "Was there anything out of the ordinary that you noticed?"

Candy took a breath and looked about the room. "I'm sorry, I don't think so. I was too busy with the massive crowd of people who barged in when I opened the doors that I didn't have time to think about anything not being normal because I had to go open the stage doors before they all squashed each other. I'm sorry. Do you think that the person who did this might have still been in the theatre with me? Might have been in the audience? Or hiding out waiting for us all to leave? Oh god, do you think if I got in through the window quicker then Keith might still be alive?"

"No, Candy, I don't think that, and you shouldn't either. We won't know how long Keith had been there until the autopsy has been done, but please try not to think about the what ifs." Annie stood and took their empty glasses back to the kitchenette, a creeping sensation tickling the back of her neck.

They were up there alone in Keith's apartment, Swift had no idea, no one knew where they were, and there was a potential killer still on the premises. Not wanting to startle Candy, Annie slipped her phone from her pocket and called the DI.

"Annie, look my signal is crap, keeps coming and going, where are you?" Swift answered almost immediately.

"I'm with Candy, the young girl from the show; we're up in Keith, Gabriel's, apartment. Door's at the back of the stage, behind the curtains and past the boxes."

"Stay put, uniform has just arrived on the scene and they're doing a sweep," said Swift. "Are you both okay?"

"As can be expected, yes, you?"

Swift's voice crackled on the other end of the phone.

"The theatre is clear... a little more relaxed about it. Annie... on high alert, for all we know the person who did this to Mirage could still be in the building. Officers will be up there as soon as they can."

"Swift, there's something else," Annie said, watching Candy curl up on the sofa from across the room. "Mirage had a son. A young boy called Benjy who's currently asleep in his room up here with us."

Swift blew out a whistle through his teeth. "Okay, thanks... team to search... next of kin."

"Who would want to do something like this, Swift?" Annie asked, straining to hear what Swift was saying. "It's not like Mirage had money, from the looks of it."

"See what info you can get from Candy while you're up there," said Swift. "... not a suspect yet so you don't need to record what she's saying or read her rights. But make sure you document... And keep an eye on Benjy, we don't want him sneaking downstairs and seeing..."

"I don't think we need to worry about that, now," said Annie, pushing away from the counter and heading towards the boy standing in the doorway. "He's just appeared. I'd better go."

"... careful, Annie, I'll be with you as soon..."

But Swift's words were drowned out by a blood curdling scream that made Annie's skin feel like it had loosened and was sliding from her bones.

FOUR

IF THERE WAS A SOUND THAT WAS HARDER TO IGNORE than a child's cry, Annie hadn't heard it.

But this wasn't just a cry pounding out of Benjy's stretched open mouth, it was visceral; so visceral Annie could taste it on her tongue, feel it in her throat.

With shaking hands, Annie pocketed her phone and pulled a smile on her face. "You must be Benjy?"

The young boy stared at her with wide eyes streaming with tears. His cheeks were flushed with sleep, his hair mussy on top of his head.

"Hiya Benjy," Candy pulled the door wider and knelt in front of him, her arms out. "Couldn't sleep?"

Annie hadn't even noticed the girl get off the sofa, her gaze so glued to Benjy, her ears aching with the screeching sound that was now turning croaky.

Benjy scuttled through the door and gripped a hold of Candy like a limpet, her shirt clasped in his hands. "Why's she here, Candy?"

"Who's here, kiddo?" Candy looked to Annie, lifting Benjy up into her arms, her thin legs shaking under his weight. Sitting with a thump back on the sofa, Candy wrapped Benjy in a blanket around his shoulders and rocked him on her knee.

As quietly as she could, Annie made her way across the living room and sat gently on the sofa opposite.

"I don't like her, she's evil," Benjy said, hiccupping tears and burrowing his head into Candy's shirt.

Annie took a moment to glance around the room just to triple check that the young boy was definitely talking about her. It was empty, besides her and the kids. He was talking about her.

"Who do you think I am, Benjy? My name is Annie and I work with the police so I'm the opposite of evil really." Annie wasn't sure if that was true, but she was going with it for Benjy's sake.

It seemed to work. He looked at her, side-eyed from the safety of Candy's lap, his brow so knotted that he looked like an old man.

"Raven, you are Raven." The boy tucked his head back into Candy's shirt.

"I'm Annie," Annie said again, lightly. "Annie Appleforth O'Malley. Who is Raven? Is she someone you don't like?"

Benjy peered out again, a twinkle in his eye. "Is Appleforth your middle name?" He was biting back a smile.

Annie shrugged. "What can I say? My parents were a little different."

That was putting it mildly, but Annie didn't think Benjy would be up for hearing about her undercover police officer parents and the history behind their breakup and subsequent disappearance of her dad and sister. That could be a bedtime story for another day.

Benjy gave a giggle. "Appleforth is a silly name."

Kids always said it how it was, and Benjy wasn't wrong. Annie hadn't spoken that name in years, it must have been the shock that loosened her tongue. She was about to change the subject back to Raven when the door crashed open and Swift burst in, his fists raised.

"Annie, what happened?" He was panting, his chest rising and falling with the speed of someone who'd just run up the stairs. "I heard a scream and then you went silent. I thought…"

He clocked the others in the room and relaxed his arms, joining Annie on the sofa.

"It's okay, Swift," said Annie. "Come and join us, Benjy here was just telling us about what scared him. Weren't you Benjy. This is DI Swift, he's a police officer too, you can trust him."

"She's called Appleforth," Benjy said, giggling. He was still wrapped in Candy's arms, the blanket around his shoulders. His eyes looked heavy.

Swift snorted. "This is Annie O'Malley."

"Annie Appleforth O'Malley," Benjy laughed.

Annie could feel Swift's eyes boring into her.

"Yes yes," Annie said. "But you weren't scared because of my middle name, were you?"

"It's pretty scary," Swift whispered.

Annie ignored him.

"Your hair." Benjy had regressed to a scared young boy again, hiding in the arms of someone he trusted.

Annie was trying really hard not to be offended by the way he was picking her apart little by little. He was a child. But he was going after her hair now, was her middle name not enough? Unconsciously she patted her head, feeling the escaped springy waves under her hands. Swift was still looking at her, she could feel the heat of his stare.

"Did my hair make you scared?" she asked, bracing herself.

Benjy nodded. "I thought you were Raven. Her hair is big and orange too."

Annie preferred auburn, but in some lights the red was overpowered by the ginger, and no one could argue that it was a large head of hair.

"Who is Raven, Benjy?" Swift asked. "Is she as scary as Annie Appleforth?"

Benjy gave a small smile and nodded his head. "Way scarier."

"Wow, no wonder you screamed." Swift moved his weight, so he was perched at the edge of the sofa, head in his hands facing Benjy. "And did you think that Annie was Raven because of her hair?"

Benjy nodded.

"So is Raven a bird with a big bouffant, like the name might suggest? Or is Raven a person?" Swift mimicked a *big bouffant* with his hands haloing around his head, before propping them back under his chin.

Benjy laughed again; a belly laugh that was contagious to all those in the room with him.

"Raven is a person. She sometimes comes to watch the show and Daddy tells me to look out for her."

"Because she's scary?" Annie asked.

Benjy nodded. "I think so. She doesn't talk to me. But that's because Daddy and Raven don't like each other."

"What makes you think Raven doesn't like your Daddy?" Annie asked, her heart breaking with pain for Benjy at the thought of his father lying dead on the stage below them.

"They shout at each other."

"And have you seen Raven recently?" Swift asked, pulling his shoulders back and sitting upright with a crunch of bones.

Benjy bit his lip and looked at the threadbare carpet lining the floor.

"You're not in any trouble, Benjy, you can tell these nice people." Candy squeezed Benjy in her arms, her eyes glistening with tears.

"Daddy told me to go back to bed and I fell asleep," Benjy said, playing with the buttons on Candy's shirt.

"That's right," Candy replied. "When your daddy has a show, you stay up here don't you? Just in case the audience want to watch you instead of daddy. And who wouldn't want to watch you, Benjy?" She tickled his belly and the boy laughed.

"When did daddy tell you to go back to bed? Was that this evening?" Swift asked.

Annie could sense that there was something the boy wasn't telling them. The way he sucked in his lips and wouldn't catch their eyes.

"It's okay, Benjy," she said. "We are only asking so we can make sure we can look out for Raven too. We can be a Raven gang, except we try to find her, not that we *are* her."

Annie closed her mouth; Swift was better at talking to children than she was.

"I was hiding in the wings," Benjy said, his childhood of living in a theatre showing in his language. "I only wanted to watch Daddy get the stage ready because when he does that, he sometimes says naughty words. Once he squashed his fingers in his vanishing cabinet and he said the f word."

"What about tonight," Annie asked. "Did he say any naughty words tonight?"

Benjy shook his head. "He was boring. He didn't take his time and he didn't notice me. He always notices me and then he chases me until he catches me, and we have a race up the stairs. I always win. I'm faster than Daddy."

"I bet you are," Annie said. "Did your daddy not want to race last night?"

"Daddy didn't want to do anything last night." Benjy sat upright, his little shoulders pulled back, his chest pushed out. "It was because she was there. She always ruins things."

"Raven?" Swift asked.

"Stupid Raven." Benjy nodded. "I stayed in the wings even after Daddy had gone back up to his room to get ready. I saw her. She was there on the stage pretending to be Daddy."

Benjy scrunched up his face and turned pink.

"Pretending to be your daddy?" Annie said, smiling. "Does Raven do magic too?"

"She's rubbish," Benjy shouted. "Daddy says she steals his ideas and that if I see her, I need to tell him. So, I went to tell him, but he sent me to bed and then I fell asleep and forgot and when I woke up, she was here."

"But it was me in your living room, so you're safe," Annie said, softly.

Benjy looked at her quizzically, as though weighing up the possibility that this Raven imposter was as scary as the real thing.

"I thought it was Raven." He kept looking. "I fell asleep. I need to tell Daddy. He told me I have to tell him if I see Raven and I did see her. She was here."

"It's okay, sweetheart, we'll make sure that we let him know Raven was here." Candy rubbed Benjy's back, chewing the inside of her cheek.

34

"Shall we get you back to bed before anyone else arrives?"

Candy nodded at the door and Annie heard the footsteps. The officers were here and sweeping the flat, and if they didn't get Benjy out of this room then he was bound to see them.

"Good idea," Swift got to his feet, obviously thinking the same. "Why don't you go and show Candy some of your favourite toys and we'll come and talk to you again soon?"

Benjy's eyes widened. "Daddy says I'm not allowed to play with my toys when I should be in bed, not except Big Brown Teddy because he is always in bed with me."

"Let's call this evening an exception, shall we? Annie, hold off for two minutes while we look in his room." Swift didn't wait for an answer, he crossed the small space in a few steps and disappeared out the door.

"I've got a water pistol, let's play with that." Benjy had come to life, shifting around on Candy's knee he hooked his fingers into a gun shape and pretended to blast her with water. "Pew pew. You're going to be all soaky."

"Maybe we should stick to the cuddly toys, hey Benjyboo?" Candy lifted him from her knee and sat him on the sofa next to her.

She had shrunk in size from the gregarious young woman who'd batted a can of drink from Swift's hand to a teen girl who probably just wanted to go to bed.

Annie mouthed *thank you* at her before adding. "There's someone on the way who can take over. We just need to wait for them to arrive. But if you need to be…" Annie didn't want to say 'heading off' and panic the young boy who was soon to be set adrift in a world with no father, but Candy took her cue.

"It's okay," she said, stifling a yawn. "Benjy and I love playing, don't we Benj?"

Benjy slithered down from the sofa and bounced across the living room floor; tiredness long forgotten. When Swift poked his head around the door and nodded all clear, Candy started to chase the boy through the room and out towards his bedroom. Their happy squeals echoed around the corridors.

Swift came back, sitting down heavily on the sofa next to Annie. "Page and Tink are waiting downstairs for Evans, he's on his way. We should go down too."

Evans was the pathologist, a teddy bear of a man with pink hair and a love of sugary confectionary. Come across him down a dark alley and he's likely to scare, but Annie had grown fond of the man who spent most of his time with the dead. He was calm and methodical and had an appetite for the truth the same as Annie and her team.

Swift rose again with some difficulty and held out a hand. Annie took it gratefully.

"There's just one thing," Swift said as they passed the uniformed officers in the hallway and made their way back to the throngs of the theatre.

"If you mention my middle name again, Swift, I

will have to disown you, and then who would solve this case? It's a family name, okay?"

Swift cocked his head to the side and let Annie go first into the wings. "Fair point…" They passed the body of Mirage and jogged down the stage and back out into the foyer. "But was the family member it was taken from, the beloved pet dog?"

FIVE

"WHOSE IDEA WAS IT TO HAVE A BUSMAN'S HOLIDAY as a night out?" Tink stood with her hands on her hips studying what was in the fridge behind the bar.

The uniformed officers had swept the foyer and asked Swift if he'd wanted them to dust for prints but the footfall that evening would have rendered the space impossible to decipher.

"Right place, right time I suppose." Swift had taken on the role of SIO and was in charge of the scene. "Or wrong place, wrong time given we were all supposed to be off for the evening."

"I was supposed to be looking after Gran this evening," Page said, hovering at the door to the theatre. "Paid for a night sit service and everything. Now I can't even sit and eat popcorn and shout 'he's behind you' for the privilege."

DC Tom Page lived with his Gran who had taken him in as a young boy and given him the steady family he'd needed to claw his way out of what could have been a very different teen-dom. She was living with dementia, and it was Page's turn to look after her now.

Tink grabbed a bag of Revels and threw them at the young DC who luckily had reactions of a cat and caught them before they flew out of the theatre doors and onto the pier. She hopped up onto the bar and made herself comfortable.

"That's the panto, you tool," she said, ripping open a bag for herself and offering one to Annie. "This was supposed to be a magic show."

Annie took a few and popped them in her mouth, chewing thoughtfully to an array of orange and toffee as Swift looked like he was about to blow a gasket.

"And it's now a crime scene so I don't know why you've all lost your sense of decorum," he said, cheeks pinkening.

"Calm down, guv," Tink replied, offering the open bag to the DI. "I don't work well on an empty stomach, and I had to leave my own stuff in the theatre while I was herding everyone out. It's not like the perp will have handled the Revels before he went and... actually, do we know how Mirage died?"

"Not death by Revels," Page muttered under his breath. "Even though the coffee ones make me want to vomit."

Swift threw his hands up in dismay and dropped them in the open bag of sweets still proffered by Tink.

"If you can't beat them and all that. Do we know Evans' eta?"

Page shook his head. "He's traveling from home, not the hospital, but I've no idea where he lives."

"South, I think," Annie said. "So he shouldn't be too long. Do you know which side of the border we're on here, Swift? We're very close to Suffolk so can we even call this one ours?"

Half of her was hoping they could leave it to the locals if the locals weren't them. But they were here now, they had seen it unfold, and they'd gotten to know Candy and Benjy.

Tink scrunched up her empty packet and hopped down from the counter. "Definitely Norfolk now, but the borders were changed back in the fifteen hundreds so some devout fans of the divide might argue the toss. Shall we go and collect what we can from the scene?"

Swift shook his head. "I know we've already been in there, but we need to wait for Evans and the coveralls. The scene is so new that we don't want to risk contaminating it more than it already is. Direct orders from Robins, those ones."

Robins was their boss. A DCI and a very good one at that, though Annie wondered if she was missing a trick this time. With the scene being so new they might find evidence that would not be there by the time Evans arrived. Transient environmental evidence; temperatures, blood colour, smells. Smells.

"There was something in the air when I followed Candy backstage earlier. I can't quite put my finger on what it was, but it made me stop and sniff." Annie was kicking herself. She knew the scent; she just couldn't put her finger on it.

"Death?" Page asked.

"Love?" Tink asked.

"Not helpful guys, but neither," Annie said, smacking her lips together. "It's… like… why is it so hard to describe a smell? Like autumn and the North Norfolk steam train."

Swift laughed. "Specific."

Tink circled back around the bar and flipped open the lid of the bin. "Like the tangy, smoky, metallic scent of firecrackers?"

Something flicked on in Annie's brain that drew her right back to high school and the smells that always used to follow the boys around.

"That's it, how did you know?"

"Guv, I think I've found something," Tink said, looking down into the bin at an empty firecracker packet.

"Bag it," Swift said.

"With what?" Tink replied and Swift rolled his eyes.

"Sorry, forgot we started off the evening as a team night out," he said. "Let's not touch anything else until Evans arrives with the stuff. Unless any of you carry around evidence bags and gloves with you on your evening off? Annie, you look like you could barely carry your keys in that thing."

Annie looked down at her glittery cross body bag. She'd forgotten it was there. It felt like a lifetime ago she'd been getting ready for what she'd thought was a date. Annie gave a small laugh and popped open her bag, drawing out her phone and her keys and a small lipstick. Underneath those was a pouch for emergencies holding gloves, bags, and a small pair of tweezers. She pulled it out and passed it to Tink.

"Thanks, Mary Poppins," Tink said, snapping the gloves over her hands and using the tweezers to lift and bag the firecracker wrapper. "The bin is empty bar this, so we should take the whole thing with us, eventually. Might be traces at the bottom."

"Noted." Swift was chewing his lip. "Annie, do you think it could be Raven? Came in here, popped a few firecrackers to knock Mirage off his feet and then?" Swift drew a finger across his neck. "Is the world of magic really that cutthroat?"

"Who's Raven when he's at home?" Page asked, pulling the door closed as the wind had picked up and was blowing a freezing chill across the foyer.

"She," Annie corrected. "Raven is another magician who Benjy thought had beef with his dad. Saw her backstage earlier this evening."

"*Said* he saw her," Swift added.

"You doubt him?" Annie asked.

"I'm not sure, but what is he, five maybe and it's the middle of the night."

42

"It's nine pm," Annie replied.

"God, feels like much later." Swift ran a hand through his hair and puffed out his cheeks. "Look, guys, I'm really sorry for dragging you out here this evening and ruining your nights. I feel like a prized idiot."

Annie put a hand on Swift's arm. "You didn't know this would happen. Unless you offed him yourself. Did you kill Mirage, Swift?"

"No," Swift laughed. "No, I didn't."

"Well then stop taking all the credit and let us do what we're paid to do," Tink replied, handing Swift the bagged evidence. "Wait, we are getting paid for this aren't we? Overtime. Time and a half. Maybe even double time because this jumpsuit isn't easy to work in."

Tink's colourful jumpsuit looked comfier that some of Annie's pyjamas, so she raised an eyebrow.

"You'll get a pat on the back and a well done and you should be grateful." The voice made them all turn to the doors and the welcome site of the team pathologist. "Right, where do you want me?"

"DO YOU WANT THE GOOD NEWS OR THE BAD NEWS?" Evans craned his body upright and pulled down his mask.

The team had watched from the stage as Evans had meticulously looked over the body of Gabriel

Mirage, taking samples and photographs and documenting everything he could without disturbing the body.

"Give me something good," Swift said, stepping up next to the pathologist.

"It wasn't magic that killed your man, here," said Evans. "So, we should be able to gather some solid, non-imaginary evidence."

"Great." Swift was deadpan. "Is your bad news as flaky as the good?"

Evans held a hand to his heart in mock shock. "Swift, you wound me. And no, it's bona fide bad news because whoever did this tried to cover their tracks and I'm worried they've managed to torch a lot of the good stuff."

"Torch?" Annie asked, not aware of any fire damage to the body.

"Someone has let off a firework in the cabinet from the looks of it, not fire exactly, but the fumes and the smoke will diminish any fingerprints and blood samples. And the aluminium oxide will tarnish the scene. Plus, there's the heat which makes it hard to determine time of death exactly, and…"

"Right yes we get it," Swift said, an eyebrow raised. "Scene is crap, evidence ruined. It was firecrackers, by the way."

"Not quite what I said, but yes in effect." Evans rolled his shoulders. "Interestingly, I would have expected the firecrackers to have done more physical damage to the body, but they must have been extinguished pretty quickly."

"That's weird. So, you think whoever did this maybe didn't mean to light them and put them out immediately?" Annie asked.

"Either that or your guy did it himself while he was still alive," Evans nodded at Mirage. "I've done what I can for the moment. I'll get the body transported to the lab and do the post mortem."

"Any ideas what killed him?" Annie asked. "Initial ideas anyway."

"Not yet." The pathologist shrugged. "His eyes are a mess, but they're not pushed in far enough to cause damage to the brain. His fingertips are bloody, could be from the perp in which case we'll have a good sample of DNA. There are no obvious signs of trauma, eyes notwithstanding, and no other wounds that I can see so far. I'll run tox, but until I get him open, I can't give any indication."

"Thanks Evans," said Swift. "Let us know as soon as you've got any useful information."

"Like if he's got any rabbits hiding in his jacket?" Evans winked at Annie, pulling off his gloves and getting out his phone to call the morgue transport.

Annie glanced around the stage, it had all been photographed now, with the uniformed officers ready to take the smaller props with them to the lab when the scene was released. There wasn't much else to see besides the large vanishing cabinet that Mirage had rolled out of. Annie moved over to look at it closer now she was dressed appropriately in a coverall. It was a large piece of furniture, wooden, ornate like it belonged in a stately home to house Victorian dresses and not dead magicians.

With gloved fingers, Annie opened and shut the doors with no sound. Something this old and solid should make creaks and groans but it was well oiled and cared for. A cast iron gate-latch set secured the doors together, with a handle on the inside to allow Mirage to come and go safely. Normally. Something had stopped him escaping this time around.

"Do you think he was dead when he was put in here?" Swift asked, mirroring her thoughts.

She thought for a moment, turning the scene over and over in her mind. "I don't think he could have been dragged in here as a dead weight. When he fell out, he fell. He wasn't tucked into a small ball; he toppled as though he'd been standing." A creep tickled up her neck and she pulled the doors wider, staring at the wood on the inside. "Look, Joe."

"Oh god," Swift said, noticing what Annie was pointing to.

On the insides of the wooden doors were scratch marks. No, that was the wrong word for them, they were claw marks. Mirage had scrabbled at the door, unable to get out, possibly unable to see at this point too. He'd been panicked and trapped. He'd also been alive when he got in the vanishing cabinet.

"So, what killed him? Given that the doors were

closed and there is no room in there for anyone else," Annie asked, rubbing at her arms.

"Maybe Evans was wrong." Swift closed the doors softly and looked down at Annie. "Maybe it was magic."

SIX

"TINK, PAGE, GET BACK TO THE STATION AND START looking into Raven." Swift was in full-on work mode now. "I also want a list of everyone who was here at the show tonight and everyone who might wish Mirage harm. And have a look into the magic community around here, Norfolk and Suffolk, and see if there's any discontent between the factions, if there are factions. Call Annie if you get anything, my signal is shot."

"Boss." Page gave a salute and he and Tink bustled out the theatre together each trying to get to the foyer doors first.

'They're like a pair of naughty siblings those two," Swift muttered, his attention back on the vanishing cabinet. "Annie, what else do you see from this cabinet?"

Taken a bit by surprise, Annie drew her gaze away from Tink and Page and to the torture chamber of

Mirage's last moments. She ducked her head inside, taking in the hollowness of the space. "It's not very large, in fact, it looks smaller inside than it does from outside."

"Yes." Swift started walking around the cabinet, knocking on the walls at the front and the sides.

Shave and a haircut.

Shave and a haircut.

The eerie echoes of the knocks made Annie's skin crawl, bouncing off the walls of the theatre with its good acoustics and far-reaching corners. Her fingers itched and she couldn't help but knock out a *two bits* reply, but where her closed fist hit the wood there was a dull thud. Annie tried again, hitting hard against the back of the cabinet.

"Here," she said, Swift already by her side. "I think it's a false wall."

The DI nodded. "That's what I was thinking, a reverse Tardis."

They walked around to the open doors and peered into the darkness. "Torch?" Annie said, flicking on her phone torch in the hope that the inside would be as well-kept as the outside. She didn't want any spiders falling into her hair.

It was empty, much as Annie would have imagined it to be. Not varnished on the inside, the wood was rougher, just looking at it Annie could feel the splinters she was about to get by climbing in. There was what must have been a fake wall all the way across the back of the cabinet, blending in so well that from the outside there was no way to tell it wasn't real.

Annie stepped into the space and held her breath, trying not to think about the last time someone was in here. Trapped inside with no escape and no way to see what was going on, Annie could feel her chest constrict and her throat start to close.

"Whatever you do, keep that door open," she said to Swift, feeling her hair start to sweat again.

"We're not in Narnia now," he whispered, widening the doors as far as they would go and looking around for something to prop them with, settling on a stool and his own bag. "You're safe."

Though Annie may mistake her boss's intentions towards her a lot of the time, she had never felt anything but safe in his presence. He was her grounding force, a comfort blanket in a nightmare, an anchor in an unruly sea.

She turned, facing what they thought was the fake wall, and started to feel her way up and down the edges.

"How are things, Annie?" Swift said, his voice sucked up by the warm wood.

"Not sure," she started. "Feels normal at the moment, but I've no idea how these contraptions work."

Thankful for her gloves, Annie could feel the wood moving and crumbling beneath her fingers.

"Not those things," Swift went on. "*Things*, thing. Life. Mim. Your mum."

Annie's stomach twisted and it was nothing to do with being trapped in a death chamber. At Tink's birthday party a few months back, Swift had presented Annie with a file he'd stolen from their work. It was a file all about her mum and the involvement she'd had with the undercover case that had caused her dad to flee with her sister. Annie had thought she'd dive right in and find out about what had happened to make her dad so scared that he hadn't been in contact with one of his daughters for nearly twenty years. But the file was currently burning a hole in the filing cabinet in the office that also doubled up as Annie's home.

A lot of the paperwork had been redacted, but Annie wasn't sure she was ready to know the answers now she had the information to hand. What if she read something she didn't like? She'd never be able to turn the clock back and unread it. Annie already knew her mum had killed a man, and that was hard enough to deal with. But then again, so had Annie, and maybe she needed to cut her mum some slack. Maybe it was the job. Or maybe her dad had been right, and her mum was someone to be feared. Annie had never had a close relationship with her, perhaps deep down she always knew there was something to fear.

"Oh, you know, good." There wasn't anything else to add. Swift had broken the law to try and help Annie and she'd shoved his help between the files of two teenager delinquents that she'd treated as a psychotherapist in another life.

"Annie?" As well as being her rock, Swift could also read her like a book.

Annie kept moving her hands up and down the fake wall, methodically feeling for any buttons or switches or small holes or anything that would mean she could break open the space and hide behind the wall and pretend she wasn't there anymore.

"Honestly?"

"Always."

"Okay, well Mim is being weird with me. She came over for Easter Sunday and gave me a Cadbury's Creme Egg and a hug but that's as much as I've seen her recently. She's probably embarrassed because she tried it on with you to get the information on Mum. Maybe she knows I know what she did, but she can't talk to me about it because that would mean her telling me she knew all about Mum's file."

"And was there information in there that Mim needs to know about? She is your sister. It's her mum too."

Annie shuffled over slightly, her fingers feeling along the last section of the fake wall.

"Um, about that," she said, her brain starting to whirr. "I haven't actually opened it yet." Before Swift could reply, Annie's brain clicked into gear, and she span around to face him. "When Mirage gets in the cabinet, he's probably facing the crowd, isn't he? Waving goodbye, pulling the doors closed behind him."

Annie mimicked his actions, pretending to close

52

the doors on herself, thinking about the easiest position for a button to release the fake wall. She looked around again, eyes focussed on the space above the lintel. She reached up and ran her fingers over the ledge. They hit something, moving it over with a soft click behind her.

"Got it," she said, turning to see what had happened.

The wall was still there, but it had concertinaed in shape, giving Annie just enough space to fold it back on itself like a fan in a clever feat of engineering. Behind was another space of similar shape and size to the front of the cabinet. Annie held her phone torch out again, gliding the light over the walls darkened with blackout paint. And there, at the foot of the light, was a gas canister complete with tube snaking out the valve at the top. Something glinted behind it but before she could reach out to see what it was, Annie felt a hand on her wrist, fingers wrapping around her and tugging hard, pulling her out of the secret compartment and out of the cabinet completely.

"What? Get off me," Her heart was hammering in her throat.

"It's me, Annie, it's me. But we're not safe here. I think that whatever is in that canister is what killed Mirage. We need to get out and we need to lock down."

"Swift, wait." Annie shrugged her arm away from his grip. "There's something there, stuck to the wall. I'll be quick. I'll hold my breath."

Ignoring his protests, Annie hopped back into the cabinet and stepped carefully past the canister. Her heart was pounding so hard it was any wonder the momentum hadn't propelled her through the back of the cabinet and out onto the stage behind. She grabbed the small piece of paper in her gloved hand and backed out again, lungs bursting.

"Annie, god, your work isn't worth your life. I thought after all the cases you'd worked on already you'd realise that." Swift sounded exasperated.

Annie rolled her eyes at him and held the paper up so they could both see what she'd found.

"And I'd have thought," Annie counter argued. "That after all the cases *you'd* worked on with *me*, you'd know to let me make an informed decision that would progress the case and keep me safe."

Swift gave a noncommittal grunt.

The paper was business card sized, namely because it was a business card. Or a calling card of some sort. Annie turned it over in her hand. It was black all over, an onyx colour that rippled in the different lights as though made of oil. Embossed in one corner was the outline of a large bird: a raven. The back had simply an email address and nothing else.

"Why leave this behind?" Annie said. "It's basically saying 'hi it's me Raven and I killed your man'."

They walked together back out into the foyer and kept going until they were out onto the slatted deck of the pier. Inhaling the salty air and clearing their lungs of whatever might have been in that canister. Below them the sea raged, white tipped and sending spray up through the gaps. Annie could feel the salt water on her skin; taste it on her lips.

"What if it's like gang warfare?" Swift pondered, leaning on the railings and looking out over the sea. "They sometimes tag their involvement in gangland crimes."

Annie went to join him, feeling the spray on her face as it billowed up the struts of the pier.

"You think the magic community is as dangerous as the gang community?" Annie asked, thinking it over herself.

"Sounds stupid when you say it out loud, though, doesn't it?" Swift turned so his back was against the railings, his head tilted to see Annie. "Abracadabra isn't exactly scary."

"A little, but only because I associate magic with fluffy white bunnies and silken scarves. But maybe there is an underground scene we don't know about. No one knows about it except the magicians themselves. Maybe Mirage trod on some toes and started delving into something he shouldn't or working in places he wasn't meant to."

Behind them, Annie could hear the boots of yet more officers marching along the pier and into the theatre.

"Or maybe he crossed someone he shouldn't have. We need to find out more about Mirage and who his family are and what he did in his spare time. I'd also like to talk to someone who's recently been to one of his shows. I want to know how it starts. I want to know what tricks he did and what the final flourish would have been."

"Candy?"

Swift nodded. "Yes, but she's probably too close to it all to give the answers I need. I want it from the eyes of a punter. Do you think we can get a list of all recent ticket sales?"

"I'll see what I can do." Annie pushed away from the railings, a cold damp sensation settling in her knuckles. She wriggled her fingers to try and bring them back to life when Swift clamped his hands over hers; warm and soft.

"Swift?" Annie gazed up at him, his eyes were wide, his nostrils flared.

He leant in towards her, his breath hot on her cheek. "Annie, don't look yet, but I think there is someone watching us."

SEVEN

"COFFEE?" PAGE HANDED TINK A LARGE MUG OF black coffee so strong he had to stir it twice as fast as normal or the spoon would have stayed upright.

"Look at this," Tink said, taking the mug.

Page pulled over his chair and sat down with a thump next to his partner. He focussed on her screen, trying to decipher the strange symbols depicted. He was tired and a little grouchy and the jumble of pictures weren't helping.

While he was making the coffees, DC Tom Page had called the sit-in service looking after his gran that night to check in on how she was doing. Agitated, they told him. A little bit aggressive towards them, they'd said. Page knew his gran was none of those things, but he also knew she found new people hard to cope with. Understandably so, given she had trouble remembering who her closest family were at the best of times, let alone strangers coming into their home and trying to make her a cup of tea. He'd reminded them that his gran liked two and a quarter teaspoons of sugar in her hot drinks and three heaped dessert spoons on her night time Weetabix, and they'd answered with the same droll voices as they probably used on their clients. He was willing to bet his month's wages that his gran had gone without her supper entirely that evening.

But there was a dead man who needed him, and Tink had obviously just asked him a question as she was looking at him with more mirth than normal.

"Sorry, Tink," he said, blinking his eyes back in focus. "Just worried about Gran. I'll get my head back in the game as soon as I've finished this."

He held up his own coffee and took a sip. It was disgusting. The idea of more grains had seemed like a good one at the time. Now? Not so much.

"That's what I was just saying," said Tink, grinning. "A warning not to drink it."

"Right," Page swallowed hard. "Yes. Sorry. I'll go give it another shot."

"Another shot is not what this needs," Tink laughed at the misnomer. "Stay here and see what you can make of this, I'll go redo these."

Tink squeezed his shoulder as she got up and soon Page was left in an empty office with nothing but a bright screen for company. He pulled his chair in closer and tried to make some sense of what he was looking at.

Moving Tink's mouse, Page skipped back a few

screens to see how she'd gotten to this home screen. From the looks of it, she'd searched for Raven and Magician and Norfolk. There was a list of restaurants and a petting zoo at the top of the search page, but a few hits down was the link that Tink had clicked on. The same pictures marked out the name of the site, like a more sophisticated WingDings font.

Page clicked again and found himself on the screen he'd just left. It was nothing more than a black page with rows of these strange characters in hot pink lettering. No header. No footer. Nothing. The characters were mostly animals with a few nature vectors thrown in. Page hovered the mouse over them one by one, but they weren't clickable links.

"It's like Raven doesn't want us to come and see their show," Page said as Tink sat back in her chair, putting two nice smelling coffees on the desk.

"That's what I thought too." Tink took back her mouse and started gliding it over her screen. "But why have a page like this instead of a normal webpage with opening hours and a little newsletter pop up offering 10% off if you sign up and agree to be sent a newsletter every month which you inevitably forget about and get annoyed when your emails are full of companies whose 10% off you didn't even use?"

Page snorted. "Personal experience there, Tink?"

"Hmm, maybe," Tink replied, her eyes twinkling.

They went back to the website and Tink continued

in her quest to cover the site with her mouse, just in case.

"Is your gran doing okay?" Tink asked, eyes on her screen.

Page shifted in his chair. He loved Tink like a sister, loved his team, loved his work, but he tried as much as possible to keep the two worlds he inhabited apart. He didn't want MCU to think he wasn't up to the job because he had outside commitments. He knew Tink had no dependents, Annie had a pot plant and Sunday the cat, and Swift just had a bit of an attitude that Page imagined took up a lot of his spare time. If he was going to be the one with the outside burden, he'd always get looked over for cases. Not that this had happened, of course, but Page knew he had one shot to make a go of this job, and he would do anything he could to make it work.

'Yeah, she's fine," he said, blowing on his coffee. "She's asleep now, nothing for me to do so I may as well stay, if that's okay?"

Tink took her eyes off the screen and her mouse arrow and raised an eyebrow. "I wasn't giving you permission to leave," she joked. "I just wanted to check she was okay because you looked a bit worried earlier."

"Yeah, thanks *boss*," Page replied, sarcastically.

"I am the most senior officer here." Tink flipped her collar and cleared her throat.

"Not for long, DS Lock," Page said, smiling.

Tink spun her chair to face him. "Oh my god,

you're going for Sergeant, aren't you? When's your exam?"

It was a well-known secret that Page had put in for his Sergeant's badge, he just hadn't openly talked about it to anyone except Swift in case he jinxed it.

"It's on Friday," he replied, trying not to count the days and hours until he'd be sat in an exam hall with a paper he wasn't allowed to turn over until he was given permission. The very thought made him feel sick.

"You're going to ace it, love," Tink said, with no sarcasm now. "You've been doing a Sergeant's work for the whole time you've been in the MCU. It's just a formality."

It may have been a formality for Tink, but Page was bricking it. He was about to tell her just that when a flash of green caught his eye.

"Stop moving." He grabbed Tink's hand over the mouse and held it still.

"Oh Page, I never knew you liked me like that," Tink snorted.

Page held his hand over Tink's, and as slowly as he could he moved the mouse millimetre by millimetre around the screen. "I hate to break it to you, Tinkerbell, but you're not my type." The mouse flashed green again. "Look, here, a link."

They pressed the mouse together and the screen lit up in a flash of confetti and eerie music and a banner with three words written on it.

"What the…" Page whistled through his teeth. "Who the hell are The Veiled Order?"

The confetti died down and the homepage came into view. The Veiled Order was splashed across the top of the page in blood red writing; underneath was a group photograph of several magicians. They were set out like a whole school photo, three rows of black top hats and tails with red splashes. In the middle, at the front, was a woman whose outfit outdid them all. She was hot pink sequins and coat tails made from what looked like peacock feathers.

"Look," Tink tapped the screen with her finger, hitting the face of a man who had been crossed through with a cross of blood red that matched the title. "That looks like Gabriel Mirage."

Page leaned in. "You're right, it is him. Can you go back to the weird first page?"

"What, why?"

"Trust me, I have an idea."

Tink blew out a breath and clicked the back button.

"Yes, look." This time Page tapped the screen. "These three lines of characters match the three lines of people in the photo." Page moved his finger along the characters and stopped at three horizontal wavy lines. "Mirage."

"Gabriel Mirage," Tink agreed. "And look at the one in the middle front, a flame with a halo, who do you reckon that is?"

"Burning angel?" Page hazarded a guess and Tink laughed.

"Probably. So do we think then that the woman on the back row second from the left is our Raven?"

The eponymous bird was the symbol in that position, so Page figured it was a good a guess as any. "Could very well be. Let's look."

"Erm, can you remember where the entry button was?" Tink laughed.

It didn't take them long to get back into the Veiled Order and when they did, Raven was waiting.

"She's rather attractive," Tink said, zooming in on the woman at the back.

Raven, if it was Raven, was nothing like her namesake. Her hair was so orange it was like a fire, her skin pale as porcelain. Her outfit was traditional magical wear with the very subtle addition of a feathered brim on her top hat.

Page guided the mouse over her face and hovered to see if anything happened. A pop up flashed on the screen, a close-up photo of Raven's face. Isabelle Raven.

"Any other details? Can you click on it?" Tink asked, trying to get her mouse back from Page.

"Nothing, here, have a go."

Tink tried clicking over the screen with no luck. It was like the Fort Knox of the magical world.

"Try Mirage." Page itched to get control of the mouse back, but he knew better than to usurp Tink from her own computer.

Mirage's pop up was nothing but the word TRAITOR.

"And what about this fancy, shmancy woman in the centre?" Page asked. "The burning angel."

Tink moved the mouse and hovered over the hot pink sparkles. Madame Seraphina, Captain of the Veiled Order.

Page gave a little chuckle. "I was almost right, Seraphina means fiery ones; they're high-ranking angels known for their zealous love and passion. Do you think all the cloak and daggers is supposed to make them seem like a super spooky group of people? Then this Madam Seraphina goes and camps it up with pink sequins and ruins it for the rest of them?"

Tink laughed. "She's their leader, she can wear pink sequins if she wants to. Besides, look at her face, I wouldn't mess with her."

Tink was right, Madam Seraphina may have been dressed all sweetness and light, but her eyes had the steely gaze of someone who'd lived through a lot.

"What do you think Mirage did to brandish him a traitor?" Page asked, looking again at the red cross covering the dead magician's face.

In the photo, Mirage had been wearing the same outfit he'd had on that evening. Tall hat and red waist-coat under his jacket. He looked happy in the parts of the photo that Page could see.

"No idea," Tink confessed. "But it should be fairly easy to find details of the Veiled Order online and see who Madame Seraphina is during the day. Get on the government website and look up their company details. I'm going to hunt down Isabelle Raven and see who's masquerading as a giant bird."

"So we find out who they really are and go and ask them why they killed Mirage?" Page said, wheeling back to his own desk and booting up his computer.

"Easy right?" Tink replied.

"Easy," Page said. "So why do I have the feeling that this has the potential to go very, very wrong?"

EIGHT

"WHAT DO YOU MEAN, SOMEONE WATCHING US?" Annie whispered, her legs turning to jelly. "Swift, maybe it's just the uniforms, or the kids up in Benjy's room."

Swift casually slotted an arm through Annie's, guiding them both back towards the entrance to the theatre. Annie felt like her head was swimming, as though the violence of the sea under the pier was shifting the wooden structure and swaying her back and forth.

"Pretend I said something funny and laugh," Swift whispered. "They won't know we're on to them if we act normal."

Annie felt a bubble of panic induced laughter pop in her throat and burst out her mouth. "Well, if they do know us then they're gonna know we're on to them if I start laughing at your jokes."

It was Swift's turn to giggle. "Oy, you cheeky sod."

They rounded the theatre door and snuck back inside, Swift closing it behind them. The foyer was busy with the forensic team finishing up their collection of the body. Hazmat had taken the canister and the scene had been cleared as safe. Despite the people, Annie shivered, rubbing her arms to try and warm them.

"What did you see?" she asked.

Swift popped his lips, glancing towards the door. "There was someone out there on the pier with us."

"It's public land though, could have been anyone."

"They didn't seem like a rubber necker," he said, shaking his head. "They were just standing there, staring at the two of us. And weirdly, dressed all in black."

Annie felt her chill dissipate with his words. "I think you might be spooking yourself, Joe. It was probably press caught on to the death, it's not like what's happened here this evening will be a secret given the amount of mobile footage I imagine is already all over Twitspace or ShiteTok."

Swift drew a hand over his mouth, scratching his stubble before shaking out his arms.

"Yeah, maybe you're right," he said, but Annie wasn't feeling it. "Maybe you're right. Shall we just have one last sweep of the place and then head off?"

"Plan, Stan," Annie replied, giving Swift's arm a

nudge. "Do you think Benjy and Candy are still around?"

Swift nodded. "Family liaison are up there now, so let's stay on the theatre level. We can delve into Keith's life later, but for now I'd like to see where Mirage comes to life."

"That's an unfortunate turn of phrase there, Swift." Annie winced, then laughed as Swift screwed his face up.

"Christ," he said. "Can't take me anywhere. Sorry."

"Shall we?" Annie gestured to the theatre, through the double doors and back to the stage of Mirage's demise.

They walked together, side by side until they reached the entrance.

"When we got here and the foyer was packed full," Swift said, stopping at the threshold. "Why?"

Annie explained what Candy had told her about the doors being locked and having to climb in through a window. About how the young girl had opened the external doors first but not the auditorium doors.

"But now I think of it, that's totally against health and safety rules," Annie said. "And this theatre isn't too old to have been built without them."

"My thoughts exactly." Swift started walking again and Annie stayed in line with him down the centre aisle towards the stage. "There's a fire exit out the side of the theatre, but that can only be opened and closed from the inside and the handle tags snap when the door is used. It's still intact, so we need to find an alternative exit, see if it's been used recently. Maybe there'll be CCTV and our job will be solved for us."

This time Annie really did laugh.

"Wishful thinking if ever there was some," she said. "But maybe there'll be some CCTV in other places in the theatre. Who would know that? Mirage ran this place by himself."

"Certainly feels like it. He hires Candy to help out on show nights but she didn't mention anyone else did she?"

Annie shook her head.

"And I can't imagine that there's a whole lot of money in magic when you're looking after a building corroding with salty sea air at the end of a rickety old pier."

They stopped at the foot of the stage. Annie felt a cold breeze circle her ankles and whip at her skin.

"Swift, can you feel that?" Annie asked.

"Feel what? The panic of my bank manager as I'm going to have to fork out for another work treat night out?" Swift was smiling.

"Knob." Annie held up a hand to stop Swift from climbing the stairs to the stage. "Cold, at your feet, can you feel it?"

"Unlike you, O'Malley," he began, "I dress appropriately for the weather."

She looked down at his jeans and boots and probably thick socks between the two. Her own ankles bare between her trendy turn-ups and ballet flats.

"Knob." She said again, dropping to her haunches and feeling around for the source of the cold air. "Look. Feel it."

The corner of Swift's mouth twitched as he dropped down beside Annie and held out his hand near hers. She could almost see the insult on the tip of his tongue until the cold air distracted him.

"Oh, yeah, I can feel it now" he said. "What is that?"

"Quite possibly the other entrance?"

"You're a genius, O'Malley," said Swift, standing back up and offering his hand. "And every day I'm thankful for your bare ankles."

Annie snorted, holding on to his proffered hand and bouncing back to her feet. "Now how do you reckon we get under the stage?"

Swift chewed his lip, looking over his shoulder and back again at Annie.

"My old school had a stage a bit like this one," he said, walking along the front, searching for something in the wood.

"Course it did."

"What?" Swift stopped and looked back at her; eyebrow raised. "Most school stages are like this one. I remember being lifted through a trap door when I played the Phantom. We had fake smoke and everything. They're awesome stages; smaller, accessible for kids, they're great for hiding in when you don't want to go to...," he stopped, edging around the corner of the stage where he looped his finger in a metal ring and pulled. A trapdoor opened beside them, the gust of frigid wind whooping around the two officers, "...maths."

Annie stepped in front, ducking her head, and throwing her phone torch back on. There was a set of three steps down into the belly of the under-stage area, which looked like it was used as storage for both the Keith and Mirage personas. She was trying to unpick the whole of Swift's sentence, but she wasn't sure where to start.

"Firstly, Swift," Annie said, moving aside a pushchair and a car seat so she could venture further in. "Not every school has a stage, let alone a theatre. For example, my secondary school had a hall which we used for gym, lunch, exams, and putting on productions of Phantom of the Opera. Incredible imagery, by the way, you in a cloak and mask surrounded by the exhalations of a fog machine. We didn't need to use a fog machine at my school, there was always a thickness in the air from the sweaty bodies and the overcooked chips."

"Nice." Swift was right behind her.

Annie stepped to the side and used her phone to check the ceiling heights before straightening up. There was enough room for them both to stand tall, and enough cobwebs dangling from the underneath of the stage to give an idea of how often Mirage would venture down here. But through the beam of her torch, Annie could see where the cobwebs trailed, knocked from their beams by a recent head or hand.

"Secondly?" Swift asked.

"What?" Annie turned and faced him.

"You said 'firstly Swift', I was just wondering if there was a secondly coming?"

"Oh, right, yeah." Annie stepped forward, following the trail of the broken cobwebs above her, and avoiding the magical detritus at her feet. "Secondly, Swift, do you really expect me to believe that you skipped maths?"

Swift laughed, sending a plume of dust and dead spiders into the air. He inhaled, sucking in a lungful, and spluttering all over the back of Annie's head.

"Oh god," he wheezed. "I think I might have just swallowed the carcass of Aragog, I can't breathe."

"Stop being such a baby," said Annie, stopping dead and looking behind her.

Swift had a hairful of webs and a face as puce as a ripe plum. He threw his hand over his mouth and his chest rippled through his coat. Eyes watering, the DI held up a finger and staggered back the way he came, leaving Annie alone in the underbelly with just the scuttling of the spiders who were still alive.

"Right, bye then Swift," she muttered, edging forwards again until she reached the back wall.

There was a mouldy cardboard box in her way, ripe with spores and sagging at the edges. Annie pushed at it tentatively with her toe but it didn't budge. She tried harder, moving it with the edge of her ballet flat until it started to slide out the way. Through the lid she could see a thick layer of dust, and underneath that a jumble of box files, some open and empty, some rammed so full of documents they wouldn't close.

Annie made a mental note to get these picked up by uniform after she'd finished down in the dungeons. But for now, she was busy. She'd found the door. Shivering, Annie pulled her coat tighter and took in what was in front of her.

The door was shorter and narrower and altogether smaller than a normal external access. Its edges weren't square with the frame and Annie could hear the whistling of the wind as it was forced through the small gaps. She could hear the battering of the waves as though they were hammering at the door to be allowed in. Thinking about it, Annie figured she was at the very back of the pier, lower than the wooden decking, down amongst the struts and the metal girders holding them together. So maybe the sea *was* knocking at the door. The idea made Annie want to keep the door firmly shut, well as firmly shut as it was now, but she took a deep breath and turned the handle.

The door blew towards her, toppling her back-wards and into the box of paperwork. A cloud of dust and god knows what else mushroomed up around her but there was no time to stop and wonder what she was inhaling as the wind kept on battering. Loose debris filled the air. Sea spray coated everything with a fine, damp mist. Annie could have sworn she felt the whole pier pitch and tilt, trying to shake her out the door like an insect caught in a glass.

"Get a grip," she said to no-one, hauling herself up off the floor and battling against the wind to look through the open door.

Annie had been right, she was underneath the pier, but there was still a huge drop down to the water below. A metal staircase bordered the doorway, leading up and down, held to the pier with giant girders and smaller metal struts. Annie stuck her head out, not wanting to test the safety of the staircase with no one else around to hear her if she fell. She looked down to the metal treads as they disappeared into the waves and wondered how scary a fire must have to be for the people trapped to choose the water. She looked up to the top of the pier where the stairs stopped at a gate on the side of the theatre. The gate was open, banging around on its hinges, hitting the wall of the theatre and the latch with equal ferocity.

Someone had been down here recently; she could tell from the missing cobwebs. They must have fled up these stairs to freedom at the first opportunity. Could it be their killer? Annie closed the door and stood in the quiet for a moment, gathering her thoughts. There could be traces of evidence down here, forensic evidence that may help them find who killed Mirage.

"Swift," Annie yelled as she walked quickly back across the room to the stairs up to the stage. "Are forensics still up there?"

There was no reply. She climbed up.

"Swift," Annie yelled again, back out in the body of the theatre. "Swift?"

She faltered. The room was empty; the uniformed officers nowhere to be seen. Swift nowhere to be seen.

"Hello?" Annie could hear the waver in her voice and feel the grip of fear snaking up her throat.

There was no need to be scared, Annie knew that, but she had a familiar sense of something about to go very, very wrong. The same way she did when she woke up that fateful morning almost twenty years ago and knew that her life was about to change. Nothing catastrophic was visible, but there was something in the air that felt charged, electric, and ready to blow.

Over the heavy thumping of blood in Annie's ears she heard the click of a door and turned with whiplash speed to see the vanishing cabinet jolt shut.

NINE

"SWIFT?" QUIETER NOW, ANNIE KEPT CALLING FOR her boss, her words echoing around the huge space.

Really, she was after the reassurance that she wasn't alone in a creepy theatre at the end of a creaky pier in the middle of nowhere. Annie knew that was highly unlikely. Swift was never a stickler for rules, but he wasn't one to put his team in danger. Now the air felt still, and the theatre had the quiet calm of a place with no interruptions, Annie was left wondering where he'd gone.

"Swift, I'm sorry I said you were a baby." Annie left the trap door open and hitched herself up onto the main stage. "I was obviously joking. I hate spiders too. I'd never kill one though, always scoop them up with a glass and a piece of paper and throw them out the window of my flat. Spiders can fly, did you know that? Not fly, technically, but they spin webs and then glide on the wind on their own magic carpets. Cool, huh?"

She was filling the quiet with a chatter and it was helping calm her nerves. A throw back to being left on her own in a silent house that had once been filled with family noise. Annie had learnt that she could talk to herself and it took away some of the feeling of being completely and utterly without the help of others. She'd tried not to take it personally, the way her mum had kept her a prisoner in their little terrace and at the same time not really being an inmate herself, but it had been hard not to wonder why no one wanted to be in the same room as her.

Annie treaded across the boards, then hesitated, looking back at the trapdoor. Why would Swift be hiding in the cabinet? Why would he have shut the door on himself knowing that Mirage hadn't been able to open it from the inside? It was more likely he'd be out in the foyer chugging a bottle of water to clear the spiders in his lungs.

But there *was* someone in the vanishing cabinet, Annie could have sworn by it. What else would have shut the doors, if not a person? It's not like the wind was strong enough. Maybe it was a white rabbit, pulled from a hat, trying to make an escape from the life of a magician's showpiece. Annie laughed, the suddenness of the noise startling her.

"I'm going to open the door now." She kept talking. It was the best thing she could think of. "And if you jump out and scare me deliberately, I will personally shove the next giant wood spider I find right up your nose."

Something creaked behind the closed doors of the vanishing cabinet and Annie felt her stomach jump up into her throat.

"And if you say abracadabra or some other magical shite like that then I will close the doors and leave you there for the bloody ghost to find. Then who'll be scared of spiders? Not you, because you'll have a ghost to contend with."

She'd reached the cabinet and was still talking. Trying to eke out her words so her sentence never ended. That way Annie could leave the door shut and stay safe on the other side.

"Okay, I'm coming in." Her voice wavered as she wrapped her fingers around the latch and slowly lifted it, eyes screwed shut.

A gust of woody air greeted Annie, along with a faint whiff of Swift's favourite aftershave.

"Joe?" Annie peeled open her eyes one at a time, her heart in her throat. She was waiting for the jump scare, a fizzing of energy coursing through her veins. "Swift?"

The cabinet was empty. Annie pulled out her phone and dialled her boss, throwing it on speaker and stepping up into the cabinet again. The fake wall was open, just as they'd left it. Annie felt around just in case her eyes were deceiving her and the DI was standing right there in a new blind spot she had no idea she suffered from. Nothing. Her fingers met the same scratchy wood as before.

"Weird," Annie whispered, backing out and circling the cabinet.

The phone clicked onto Swift's answer machine and Annie left a message asking him to call her and pocketed it away again. She headed around the back of the theatre, following the path she had taken earlier with Candy. It was empty. No sign of Swift or anyone else for that matter. She tried the foyer, empty as the rest of the place seemed to be. Annie pulled open the external doors and startled a uniformed officer guarding the crime scene.

"Sorry, I didn't mean to make you jump, "she said, shivering in the night air.

"That's okay, O'Malley," the young officer replied, smiling. "I thought you'd all gone, didn't realise you guys were still in there. It's a good job I was behaving myself, isn't it? I was half thinking I might go and get myself some seaside chips, but I think the shops are all shut."

"Not sure there are any shops out here. You'll be lucky to get anything at this time of night, anyway."

"It's just eleven."

"Oh," Annie smiled. "That's the second time this evening one of us has thought it's later than it actually is. There's some sort of weird magic going on in there."

She nodded her head towards the theatre.

"Point of the show that is, Annie," the officer laughed.

"Don't suppose you've seen Swift come out, have you?" Annie asked, eyes searching the dark pier.

The officer shook his head. "Nope sorry, is he not with you? The last people to leave were the two kids."

"Where have they gone?"

An icy blast swept off the sea and whipped the officer's words from his lips. The pier rattled and shook underfoot, and Annie felt like she was going to end up in the waves below. The officer grimaced and put out a hand, bracing himself against the wall of the theatre.

"Sorry, Annie, I'm not very good with open water," he said, rather green around the gills. "Erm, I think the girl has been taken to the station to give a statement. And the young boy's mum has been located so he's heading there with the FLO."

"Thanks," said Annie, heading back inside. "And if you see Swift, can you tell him to call me, please?"

The officer nodded and Annie shut the door behind her, relishing the warmth of the foyer. The DI had to be in the theatre then. This was the only way in and out if she didn't count the door under the stage into the sea. There was no way Swift would have been able to get past her to that door without them passing each other, and there would be no reason for him to either.

"Swift?" Annie shouted again, ready to do another sweep of the whole building.

She was cold and tired and irritated and had a list of things she was going to say to him when she found him, none of them very nice. But as she rounded the stairs of the empty building and looked up into the darkness of the flat, Annie decided that she didn't mind where he was hiding as long as she found him. It was eerie.

Taking it one step at a time, Annie walked slowly up the stairs to the flat. A creeping sensation that she wasn't alone met her with each step. The skin on the back of her neck prickled, and her scalp crawled with the sensation of insects. She had the feeling she was being watched. Whipping her neck around, Annie strained to see in the darkness below. A shadow passed across the floor of the backstage, a sweeping mass of black, a cloak of darkness. But there had been no one down there. The whole building was empty. She turned and took the last few steps as quickly as possible without running, the whole time expecting someone to grab her ankle.

Slamming the door behind her, Annie caught her breath in the warm light of the flat. It smelt comforting, of bread and coffee, something Annie had taken for granted the first time around.

"Milk and one sugar, please," she said, heading on into the living area, figuring that's where Swift had set up base. "I need the energy after all the evening's excitement."

From thinking this was a date to finding a dead body to thinking Swift had vanished into the ether,

Annie needed more than coffee and sugar, but she'd take what she could. Only, when she got there the living room was empty, the kitchen was empty. Annie felt her stomach drop. She quickly worked her way through the rest of the flat. Keith's bedroom, empty. The bathroom, empty. Benjy's small, warm, loved bedroom, empty.

Standing in the hallway, the flat behind her, the door to the theatre in front, Annie pulled out her phone and dialled.

"Tink, I think we have a problem."

"Let me guess," Tink replied. "You've got too many silk hankies out and can't put them away again? You've lost your wand? Or... hold on, Page says the clowns won't get back in the mini. Page, you're still at the circus, dude. It's magic. We were at a magic show. Sorry, Annie, just can't get the staff these days."

Annie could picture the two of them back in the office, drinking coffee and feeling safe. She wanted to magic herself back there and she wanted to magic Swift there too.

"It's Swift," she started. "He's gone."

"Gone?" Tink scoffed. "Left the theatre? Left you? Left the country?"

The shoe was on the other foot. Annie was the one reporting a crime. So many times during police academy training and since re-joining the force a couple of years ago, Annie had been on the receiving end of these reports. Loved one scared about the whereabouts of their family members. Husbands or wives not able to get their words out because they were too emotional. Annie felt like that now.

"We were searching under the stage for the other exit, Swift needed some air and then... poof, gone."

The line went quiet. Annie looked at her phone to make sure Tink was still there.

"That's weird," Tink said eventually. "Swift wouldn't just walk off and leave you."

"I know," Annie said; and she did know, even if she'd doubted it for a split second, she knew he wouldn't desert her unless there was a good reason.

"Hold on, let me check something." Tink went quiet again, and Annie could hear her tapping on her phone. "Nope, still weird. We have each other on the *find me* app and Swift's is turned off. He never turns it off. Sometimes he tells me not to look at it, but he never turns it off."

"Maybe he's still got no signal," Annie said, edging back into the living room and closing that door too, cocooning herself in the safest place she could think of to hand. "What do you think is going on?"

"I don't know, Annie," Tink said. "Did he say why he was leaving, why he needed air?"

"Yeah, it was nothing really, he inhaled a spider and went to get a drink," Annie replied, her skin crawling.

"Listen, Annie, Page and I found something while we were looking into Mirage." Tink was tapping away on her keyboard as she spoke. "I'm emailing it over to you now. There's a group of magicians called The Veiled Order. Mirage had something going on with them as you'll see from the screenshot, but we found Raven too. There are a few in the Order who we're searching for as we speak, but be careful, Annie, they're a secretive bunch and we already know how deceptive they can be. I'll put out an alert for Swift and get a car back out to you. Page and I will be with you as soon as we can. We'll find him, Annie."

Annie ended the call and sank down onto the sofa. With shaking hands, she opened the email from Tink and staring back at her, amongst the pictures of the magicians, was a woman she would have recognised anywhere.

TEN

MORE THAN TWENTY YEARS HAD PASSED SINCE ANNIE had seen Madame Seraphina but she would recognise her even if it had been twenty more. It was the eyes; steely blue and penetrating, perched either side of a long, pointy nose.

Back when her parents were still together, Madame Seraphina had been known simply as Sera. She'd hang out at their house and drink teas with her mum on the prim sofa, neither woman really talking to the other, just sitting there sipping boiling drinks and staring into space. She was a different woman around Annie's dad. Loud, raucous, chugging beers and generally being a nuisance to the tranquillity of their family home. Annie could still hear the tuts from her mum at the language Madame Seraphina would use, and the slammed doors after she'd gone.

Annie could vividly remember the way Madame

Seraphina smelt of Patchouli oil, the sickly-sweet earthiness followed her through every room and trailed in her wake. She'd been the leader of a community out on the North Norfolk coast, gathering like-minded individuals to come and work the land and live in ramshackle buildings they'd taken, unasked, from farmers. Vague recollections of visiting with her dad, Annie could only see snapshots of the commune; stacked hay bales ripe for climbing, old tractors brought back to life, a barn full of mattresses and people with long hair and floaty clothes and a smell that she recognised now as weed.

Back then, Madame Seraphina, Sera, had been a frequent visitor to the O'Malley home in the weeks and months leading up to the disappearance of Robert O'Malley and his daughter, Mim. Which is why the police had spent a lot of time at the commune in the weeks and months afterwards. Though they never found any trace of Annie's father and sister, Sera had been evasive and tight lipped and had never set foot over the threshold of the O'Malley house again. Rumour around the station was that she'd hidden the pair in her commune before they moved further North to the next cult her father had joined. Though it turned out there had been no cult. So, had there been no moving North either?

Annie looked at her phone, tapping the screen back to life. Her fingers were white knuckled and tense. There she was again, Madame Seraphina. Grey haired now, but still wearing clothes that made her centre of attention. What was with the pink sequins? Annie swiped out of her emails and dialled another number.

"Annie? It's way past your bedtime, what are you doing up?" Mim sounded like she was out on the town. Through the silence pulsing in the theatre flat, the noise coming from Annie's phone was like a jack-hammer. Crowds of people. Music. Shouting. "Hold on, I'll just go somewhere quieter."

Annie waited while her sister made her way through whatever mob of people she was mingling with, until the background quietened to wind and road noise.

"Mim, sorry am I interrupting a night out?" Annie said, glad to have her sister's company even if it was just over the phone.

"No, no, just a quiet one with some friends." Mim struck a lighter and Annie could hear the way she spoke as though holding a cigarette between her lips.

A quiet night out for Mim sounded like something that Annie would have to prep for for weeks in advance, needing at least another week post night out to recover. Whereas Annie had a handful of friends she kept close to her, Mim had made quadruple that amount in the short space of time she'd been back in Norfolk. The sisters were chalk and cheese, but it was no surprise given their different upbringings.

"I won't keep you long, are you still relatively sober?" Annie asked.

Mim barked out a laugh. "Nope, but when am I

ever these days? I am a fully functioning human being even with a belly full of Cosmos. What's up?"

Annie took a breath, not relishing what she knew was coming. But she was up against the clock, Swift had been gone for almost an hour and Annie knew that with each passing second it would be harder to find him.

"I know you were too young to remember Dad kidnapping you," Annie started and Mim interrupted before she could finish.

"Rescuing me," she said, inhaling with a pop of her lips.

"Yes, sorry, when he took you away. But can I send you a photo and will you tell me if you recognise this person?"

"What are you doing Annie? It's midnight on a Friday night and you're delving into our childhood. Don't you have a life?"

The question cut like a knife.

"It's not like that, listen, Swift has vanished, and I think this person is involved somehow, I just need to know if you recognise her that's all?"

"Are you still mad at me about trying to proposition Swift for information about our mum, is that what this is?" Mim's voice was even but Annie could hear the edge she was walking. "I swear to you, sis, I don't fancy him, he's all yours if you ever work up the courage to tell him. I just wanted answers and he was the best way to get them. It might have been fun too, he's hot."

"Maybe you are too drunk," Annie replied, wanting to rip roar her anger onto Mim for doing that to her, but shouting down the phone wasn't going to help anyone right now, especially Swift.

"No, no, sorry, send me the photo and I'll see." Mim cleared her throat with a rattle of smoke congestion.

Annie dropped her phone from her ear and tapped on the screen, forwarding the picture to Mim's WhatsApp.

"It's on its way," she said, quietly.

Annie scratched at the skin around her thumbnail until it stung, waiting to hear what her sister had to say, but in the end, it was the sharp intake of breath that gave Mim away.

"You recognise her too?"

"Um…" The line went quiet.

"Mim, just tell me the last time you saw her, please? Swift could be in danger."

The way Mim laughed made Annie want to reach down the phone and grab her sister by the throat. She didn't get to ridicule Annie, not when all Annie was doing was trying to help her friend.

"Mim! God, I don't know why I bothered." Her face felt hot, and her pulse pounded in her throat.

"Sera is all bark no bite," Mim said, but Annie could hear the humour in her voice. "What the bloody hell does she look like? Those sequins are doing nobody any favours. And who the hell is Madame Seraphina?"

"Do you know where she is living?" Annie ignored the comments and pressed on trying to get information that might be useful.

"No idea, soz," Mim said. "Haven't seen her for a couple of years, last I heard she had abandoned everyone at the commune and was living in a rather lovely barn conversion near Holt on the proceeds of her followers. But I can guarantee you this, Sera is not involved in the disappearance of Joseph Richard Swift, DI."

Hearing Swift's full name from Mim's lips was the final straw. Annie ended the call and yelled in frustration, throwing her phone onto the sofa beside her. It bounced and ended on the floor with a crack.

"Oh my giddy aunt," Annie muttered, picking it up and inspecting it for damage. The screen was fine, Mirage's living room floor not so much. There was a dent in the floorboards that Annie covered with the rug. He wasn't going to mind, not now.

The thought of Mirage's body, prone on the floor of the theatre, fallen from the place of his demise in the vanishing cabinet made Annie's anger at Mim simmer gently.

"Where are you Swift?" She dialled his phone again. Straight to voicemail. "Where have you gone? Who has got you?"

She left a quick message, but no longer able to sit still, Annie dragged her tired body from the sofa and opened the door to the hallway. It was pitch black. A trickle of fear ran through her veins, icy cold and making her shiver. Annie had left the hallway light on; she was sure of it. In fact, Annie had no doubt whatsoever in her mind that when she backed into the living room earlier the hallway had been aglow with not only the overhead light, but the lights from each of the bedrooms and the bathroom too. Now, Annie couldn't tell if all the doors were open or closed because she couldn't see them. It was too dark.

"Hello, is there anyone there?" With her hands out in front of her, Annie stepped into the blackness. Her phone was at ten percent and she didn't want to waste what was left of the battery on the torch when Swift might be about to call at any minute. So, she was feeling her way to the switch by the stairwell door.

Tiredness made her limbs feel like jelly. The carpeted hallway felt like warm tarmac just laid. Something rustled in the darkness beside Annie. A soft breeze blew on her cheek. Annie couldn't breathe. She lurched forwards in the hope she was facing the right way, her hands hitting the wall opposite with a thud that jarred her wrists.

"Ow, shoot," she whispered, feeling around for the switch. "Come on, come on."

Hitting the edge of the stairwell door with her knuckles, Annie moved her hands across and found the light, clicking it and flooding the space with a warm glow. The skin on the back of her neck prickled with a warning that she wasn't alone. Slowly, Annie turned her head, knowing there was someone behind her. But when she peered out through screwed up eyes, the hallway was empty.

Letting out a long, slow breath, she looked at the doors closed tight against their surroundings. There *had* been someone else up in the flat with Annie, she knew it. Doors don't just all close on their own. She pushed one open to check it wasn't hinged. It stayed there, offering a view of Mirage's bedroom, light still on. So whoever it had been, hadn't taken the time to switch off all the lights. Why plunge the hallway into darkness and not everywhere, unless it was to give themselves cover to flee back down the stairs?

What is going on?

Annie's phone sprang to life, making her jump. She lifted it, chest filled with hope that it was Swift with a hundred and one reasons why he'd fallen off the face of the earth. It was Page.

"Tom, hi," Annie said, trying not to sound too disappointed.

"Sorry Annie," Page replied, obviously hearing the disappointment anyway. "I wanted to send this in a text, but Tink told me to call you."

"What's up?" Annie made her way back down into the theatre. She wanted to be back amongst people and the officer at the door was the only person she knew who was still around.

"We're on our way back to the theatre. We're about ten minutes away." Page was an echo and Annie knew she was on speakerphone in Tink's car.

"But we've had an update from Evans about the possible cause of death of Gabriel Mirage."

"That was quick." Annie walked quickly through the back of the theatre and out onto the stage, stopping to listen to Page.

"Yeah, it's just a prelim, but Evans said that Mirage's whole body had the cherry-red signs of carbon monoxide poisoning on his skin."

"Carbon monoxide?" Annie peered at the door to the vanishing cabinet. "Do we think that's what was in the canister Swift and I found then?"

"Probably. Tox is being run on Mirage's blood and the substance in the canister we recovered."

"So are we thinking it was accidental? What I don't get is, if there was carbon monoxide in the cabinet with Mirage and someone set off firecrackers, why didn't the whole place explode?" A shudder ran over her body as Annie pictured a very different scene, one where the whole of the MCU might have been wiped out in one mass explosion.

"That's the thing," Page replied. "Evans said that the level of CO in the atmosphere in the cabinet must have been almost one hundred percent to give such a vivid redness to Mirage's skin."

"And that level of Carbon Monoxide would mean that there would be no fire as there's limited oxygen to burn." Annie whistled. "So Mirage was poisoned in one of the worst ways possible, and blinded, in an order we're not sure of yet."

"Yeah."

The unspoken conclusion between them was like a red-hot poker that neither of them wanted to hold.

"Which means we need to find Swift, and we need to find him fast," Tink shouted across the car. "Because carbon monoxide waits for no-one."

ELEVEN

By the time Page and Tink arrived back at Wexwade Theatre, the rain had started. It poured in sheets across the carpark and hammered on the roof of the theatre like stones. The two officers looked like they'd been in a shower fully clothed as they huddled in the foyer with Annie.

"So, this is what we have got?" Tink said, firing up the coffee machine behind the bar, while Annie and Page sat on the counter. "A magic show gone wrong. Keith Stuckley, aka Gabriel Mirage, was poisoned with Carbon Monoxide, blinded, and shoved in a vanishing cabinet where he definitely didn't vanish."

"I think he was poisoned in the cabinet," Annie said. "The canister in the hidden section makes me think he was locked in the cupboard that was then filled with gas."

"Nice," Tink said, eyebrow raised.

"We also have the card of another magician called Raven found in the cabinet. Plus Mirage's son, Benjy, was told to report back to his dad if he ever saw Raven."

"And Raven was in that screenshot we sent you," Page added. "She's about your age, Annie, striking looking."

"I didn't even notice her," Annie confessed. "I was too busy trying to find out more about Madame Seraphina. I knew her when I was younger."

"What?" Tink scrunched her nose.

Annie gave them the shortened version of events, from Sera aka Madame Seraphina hanging out with her dad, to Mim's version of where she lived now.

"So what are we thinking?" Tink said. "That this Seraphina woman has a new cult full of magicians? They've killed Mirage for some, as yet, unknown reason, and left a calling card so the rest of the magical world knows not to mess with them?"

"It all seems a bit cutthroat," Annie conceded. "And we don't know that Madame Seraphina is still into all that cult stuff, sounded a bit like she took what she needed and then set up alone."

Annie scoffed, that sounded a bit like her sister and dad too.

"Page," Tink turned to the young DC while the milk frother noisily did its thing. "You're quiet."

Page chewed his cheek.

"You're thinking about Swift?" Annie asked.

Page nodded. "Magic *can* be quite cutthroat, from what I've heard, Annie."

Annie nodded and Page continued.

"If this is all to do with a magic circle secret, if Mirage was killed for knowing something he shouldn't or giving away secrets he shouldn't, then what if Swift accidentally found something out and now he's…"

Page let his words trail but they all knew what he was getting at.

"But what could he have found out in the small space of time between being under the stage with me and vanishing?" Annie wracked her brains. "It was fifteen minutes, max. And it's not as though the magic secrets were spread out over the stage for us to see, was it?"

"You found the secret of the cabinet." Tink poured out milk into three cardboard mugs and handed around the coffees.

Annie took hers, a sudden chill creeping up her neck.

"You think that secret is enough to kill for?" she said, not really expecting an answer. "You think I could be in danger too? Why didn't they take me when I was on my own under the stage? Or up in the flat?"

She remembered the feeling she'd had that she'd not been alone.

"Maybe because they didn't have the opportunity,

even though you were alone you were on the phone to us?" Page said, blowing on his latte.

"So, what do Madame Seraphina and the Veiled Order have to do with it all?" Annie asked.

"That's what we need to find out." Tink was on her phone, swiping across the screen, her brow creased. "Oh god, units are on BOLO for Swift. He's been officially reported as missing, apparently no one has been able to get hold of him."

Annie felt the room tilt around her. She felt the bile rise in her throat. She needed fresh air. Jumping down from the bar counter, she wobbled across the foyer to the front doors of the theatre and threw them open, stumbling outside and right into a figure dressed all in black.

"Hey," she shouted as the figure dropped what they had been holding and turned. "Wait."

They didn't wait. The figure started running. They fled across the slick wooden pier to the paved area where it met the road, and skipped the small railing to the almost empty car park before Annie could get her bearings.

"Page, Tink, quick," she yelled, starting to chase after the figure in black.

They rushed through the door, across the pier, and past Annie, spreading out. Tink ran around the outside of the carpark and Page hopped the railings like the figure had. Annie started up again, running as fast as she could towards the darkness at the end of the car park.

"Police," she yelled. "Stop running."

She wasn't in the mood to mess about. Annie just wanted to find Swift and make sure he was okay. She was also now worried that she was a target too, and running off by herself into the darkness wasn't a great idea. But the pounding footsteps of her team running nearby gave her the impetus she needed to keep going.

"Stop." Annie couldn't even see who she was shouting at now.

The moon was just a sliver of a nail and with the rain and cloud cover there was no natural light to speak of. With the spotlights from the carpark fading into the distance, Annie felt the ground underfoot get rough and uneven. Her ankles screamed out with every step and Annie felt herself slow as the trees reached out and grabbed at her coat and her jeans. Something caught her and she tumbled to the soaking wet floor in a heap, the rain hitting her head and streaming down her face in cold rivers.

"Annie?" Tink appeared first, followed not long after by Page, pink cheeked and out of breath. "Annie what happened. Are you okay?"

"I was too slow," Annie cried. "I was too slow to get them, Tink. What if that was our only chance. What have they done to Swift?"

Tink poked an arm through Annie's and hoiked her up from the ground.

"We need to get indoors. The cavalry is on their

way to take over the search for Swift and for whoever that was."

Tink marched Annie across the carpark and back onto the pier, Page skipping along beside them.

"Are you injured?" she asked.

Annie shook her head. "No, just cold and scared."

"You're safe now," Page shouted over the drum of rain.

"Not scared for myself, Tom, thank you though," Annie shouted back, releasing her arm from Tink's. "I'm scared for Swift. What's that?"

Annie ran up to the theatre door where a large piece of paper was trying to flutter in the wind but failing because it was too wet. She bent to pick it up, carefully as it started to disintegrate in her fingers.

"Guys," she said, drawing out the vowel. "Look at this."

Hurtling through the theatre door, the three detectives dripping all over the floor walked right into the officer who had been guarding the theatre.

"What happened to you?" Annie asked, laying the paper down on the counter of the bar and facing the uniformed policeman whose cheeks had gone a fetching shade of pink.

"I'm so sorry," he said into his collar. "I needed to pee."

"They were watching the door then?" Page piped up, shrugging out of his sopping coat. "Waiting for a gap to… what? What were they doing?"

"This," Annie

The four police officers crowded round the piece of paper left at the scene, their heads almost touching as they tried to read what was printed on it.

In a theatre filled with wonder, where illusions come to life,

A magician's grand performance, causing wonder and strife.

After the cheers have fallen, a disappearance takes its toll,

A missing person vanishes, not the magician's control.

Through trapdoors and secret panels, the magician cast their spell,

But when the curtains part once more, the mystery deepens, oh so well.

With robes of velvet, wands in hand, they vanish into air,

Leaving behind a mystery, a puzzle oh so rare.

So tell me, dear seeker, with your keen and watchful eye,

Where did the magic lead them? Solve this riddle, I do not lie.

For in the heart of wizardry, where dreams and spells entwine,

The missing person waits for you, their
fate within your mind.

"What the...?" Annie wiped droplets of water from the paper, uncovering the signature at the bottom. "The Veiled Order sent someone to the theatre to drop off a *riddle*? Do they think this is some kind of game? A man is dead. Another is missing."

Annie felt a hand on her arm and realised she had been shouting. Tink's face came into focus, the red anger dissipating around the edges of Annie's vision.

"It's late and you've not slept or, I'm betting, eaten for ages." Tink withdrew her hand. "I say we let the officers get to work on gathering whatever extra evidence they can from here, and the three of us go get some grub and some rest. We won't be helping Swift or anyone if we can't think straight and our blood sugars are all over the place."

"But..." Annie started.

Tink held up a hand. "I get that you want to find Swift. And the first few hours are crucial. But Annie, honestly, are you thinking straight, because I'm not?"

"How am I supposed to think straight? I'm reading a riddle. A riddle. Like we're back in primary school and figuring out where Supertato has been hidden by the Evil Pea."

"I don't even know if I'm awake anymore, Annie, that sentence made no sense." Tink burst out laughing and it was all Annie could do to join in.

"Stop it, it's a book, and Joe..." Annie snorted.

"Joe would want you to be fed and watered." Tink was puce.

"Guys, I don't mean to spoil the party here, but the cavalry has arrived," Page stuttered, looking at Annie and Tink with trepidation.

"More vegetables?" Annie could barely get her words out now and Tink looked as though she was about to pee.

"O'Malley, Lock, Page, update, now." DCI Robins had entered the building and was looking at the members of the MCU as though they'd sprouted two heads.

Annie wiped the tears from her cheeks with her sleeve and caught her breath, teetering between laughing and crying and not knowing which way she was about to fall.

"Sorry Guv," she said, carefully unsticking the wet paper from the bar and showing it to Robins. "This was just hand delivered to the theatre. There were signs that Mirage was killed by someone called Raven, and Raven is a part of this Veiled Order. We're not sure why they've taken Swift, or where, or how…"

Annie felt her voice trail, words escaped her.

"Well, you're in luck," Robins said, eyes narrow. "While you and your team were in here having a jolly, our patrol picked up your postman trying to escape the woods and run all the way back to Norwich. Or should I say postwoman? They're taking her to the station, and I want you and DS Lock to interview her."

Wide eyed, Annie nodded. "Yes, sorry guv, we just…"

"No excuses, off you go." Robins waved her away with a flick of her wrist.

Annie wasn't sure she could feel worse, but somehow she did. Robins had always stood by Annie, even though she wasn't a part of the actual police force, and Annie knew now she was going to have to work twice as hard to gain back her trust.

Annie turned to the youngest member of their team. "Page, can you get the officers to bag up the paperwork from under the stage? Go through it and see what it is. Mirage kept it for a reason, down there with the old baby stuff and worn-out magical equipment. It might shed some light on why the Veiled Order were so peed off with him."

"On it." Page gave Annie a salute and went to join the officers combing the building.

"Leave your car here, Annie," Tink said, holding up her keys. "I'll drive us back."

"Oh and O'Malley?" Robins shouted as they were leaving the theatre. "Be careful of these guys. Don't let them manipulate you, make sure you stay professional and on your guard at all times. They know your family and they' won't be afraid to use that against you."

TWELVE

TINK DROVE THEM BACK TO THE STATION. DESPITE the speed at which she got there and the angle at which she took her corners, Annie felt herself drift into a dreamless sleep. Jolted awake forty minutes later she wiped the dribble from her face and puffed out her cheeks.

"Rest; tick," Tink said. "Now let's raid the vending machine and gather our thoughts before we go and talk to whoever it was we were chasing."

They climbed out the car into the dark and trotted across the carpark to the station door. Annie's wet clothes stuck to her like velcro on her skin. She peeled her coat off and tried to flap out her top, but it suctioned against her with a loud slurp.

"I've got some spares in my locker," Tink said, looking Annie up and down.

"As if I'd fit in anything of yours, Tink, thanks

though." Annie was about a foot taller than Tink and a dress size or two larger.

"Well then can you go and raid Swift's locker instead," Tink went on. "He's got a pair of jeans and a jumper that his mum knitted in there."

Annie raised an eyebrow but the look on Tink's face made her keep her mouth shut. She gave a quick nod and headed in the direction of the staff changing rooms.

Ten minutes later Annie stood at the interrogation door with Tink, trying not to sniff too obviously at the mix of wool and aftershave blooming from the navy jumper she'd found in Swift's locker. She'd added her own belt to the jeans and they stayed up, just. Tink was fresh faced and in clean clothes that fit, but between them they looked a bit of a state.

"Ready?" Annie asked.

"Let's go. You gonna be good cop or bad cop?" Tink looked dead serious.

"I don't think I've ever played that game before, I've always been honest cop," Annie said, hand faltering on the door.

"Good cop it is," Tink winked at her. "Watch yourself, I get carried away."

Tink pushed the door open with a bang and Annie scurried in behind her. Pulling her shoulders back, Annie sat down and they started the recording. Tink spoke first, letting the young woman opposite know what was on the cards and Annie took that moment to properly look at the figure they had chased through the woods outside the theatre.

She was younger than Annie had expected, early twenties, maybe. A shock of orange hair fell across her shoulders. Her skin was porcelain, unblemished by spots or veins or scars or the red cheeks that Annie could feel on her own face, brought on by the cold and the rain and the emotions she was feeling. Annie recognised the woman, and it didn't take long for the cogs in her brain to click into place and remember where she'd seen her.

"Raven?" Annie said, interrupting Tink's tirade. "You're Raven? I recognise you from the website."

Raven's eyes narrowed, her brow furrowed.

"This is O'Malley, I'm DS Lock, can you give us your name and date of birth for the tape." Tink eyed Annie, a warning not to interrupt again. Tink was really getting into character. "And would you like any legal representation while you're here?"

The woman sat forward, leaning her hands on the table. Annie could see the shake in her fingers, even as she twisted them around themselves.

"I'm Isabelle Raven," she said and gave her date of birth. "And no, I don't need it, I've done nothing wrong."

Annie did a quick calculation in her head which put Isabelle Raven at twenty-seven.

"Do you know why you're here?" Tink barked.

Raven jolted on her chair, scraping the legs across the floor. The sound made Annie's teeth hurt.

"I... um, I was walking in the woods and was stopped by officers who said I had to go with them." Raven looked at her fingernails and chewed her cheek.

"That's it, is it? You were walking in the woods." Tink wasn't having any of it. "You think you were picked up because you were walking in the woods? What about Mirage? What about Swift?"

Raven looked between the two officers, her eyes red. She shook her head and bit her lip.

"Why were you running?" Annie asked. This timid woman didn't seem the sort of person who would scarper from officers. "Why not just talk to us?"

Raven looked back down at her fingers. "No comment."

"Oh great," Tink scoffed. "We've got a silent one. Okay, well let me tell you what we know, shall I?"

Tink left a lengthy silence, the tick of the clock the only sound. Raven held out for less time that Annie thought she would before looking up from her fingers at Tink.

"Oh, there you are. Raven—nice magical name by the way—really suits you. I'd have thought you'd look different, dark hair, dark eyes, but we'll go with it. You really do look more like a parrot though. Maybe that's not quite scary enough for your magic circle. They're a nasty bunch, aren't they?"

Raven's nostrils flared, a pinkness spread across her neck, rising up into her cheeks.

"We're good people." She flung a hand over her mouth and dropped her eyes back to the table.

"So good that you ostracised one of your own and then killed him. Poisoned him with carbon monoxide too, awful way to die."

Raven's eyes filled with tears but she didn't rise to the bait so Tink continued.

"Mirage would have suffocated from the inside out, you know? He would have felt the strain on his body, known he was going to die. He scratched the inside of the vanishing cabinet he was locked in, bloodied his fingers trying to get out. And who blinded him? Was that you?"

The blood rushed out of Raven's face almost as quickly as it arrived. She drew her lips into a thin line.

"We know you had arguments with Mirage," Annie said, softly. "His son was warned away from you, told to tell his dad if he saw you. Why is that? Were you a threat to the young boy as well?"

"No comment."

Annie bit down the anger rising in her. "I found your card in the secret compartment in Mirage's vanishing cabinet. Why leave a calling card? Were you acting on behalf of the Veiled Order? Did you kill him because they told you to?"

"Did you take Swift because they told you to?" Tink shouted. "I can't see you making a decision like that on your own. Or any decision, really."

"No comment." Raven was steely now, Annie didn't think the whole bad cop act was working, but she knew Tink's anger was real and there was nothing the DS could do about it.

"Swift is a good guy, Raven," Annie said. "We just need to know he's okay. Can you at least tell us that."

"I don't know if he's okay." Raven looked right at Annie. "You need to stop looking. Read the riddle."

"What about Mirage? We have reason to believe you were in the theatre before the show tonight. We have your card in the place where Mirage died. No doubt we'll have your fingerprints all over it too. It's not just circumstantial evidence, Raven. With the Veiled Order website more or less posting that they hated Mirage and wanted him dead, we have enough to charge you with his death."

Annie wasn't sure if they did have enough, but the weight behind the words brought the tears back to Raven's eyes.

"I told you. Read the riddle."

"We're not in a movie, Raven." Tink was back to shouting. "We can't just accept your *read the riddle* answer and send you off on your merry way. This is murder we're talking about. Holding someone against their will. These are serious charges that would land you a sentence that would take away the rest of your life. And so they should."

Raven chewed her bottom lip, determined not to let the teardrops fall from where they were wobbling on her lash line.

"Isabelle, if you're covering for The Veiled Order,

you need to know that they don't have your best interest at heart. No one who cared about you would put you through this. Why don't you just tell us the truth?"

A single tear tracked down Raven's porcelain skin, leaving a glistening trail on her cheek. She licked it away and drew her lips into her mouth.

"I can't tell you the truth," she said, her voice cracking. "I can't lose my family."

Annie sat forwards, resting her arms on the table between her and Raven. She opened her hands out.

"Have they threatened you? Have they threatened your family?" said Annie. "We can help you. We can protect you and your family if needed." Annie glanced at Tink who was stony faced and not giving anything away. "Please tell us where Swift is. If he's okay? We need to find him, and you'll be in a lot more trouble if anything happens to him, I can't guarantee your safety if you harm an officer so well loved."

Annie felt her own voice waver and she sat back, not wanting to let her emotions get the better of her in an interview situation.

"O'Malley is right," Tink added. "You harm one of us, you're fair game. You should see what happened to the last person we brought in who had hurt an officer."

Annie looked over at Tink. That hadn't been what she had meant by her words. Annie hadn't been threatening, had she?

"No comment." Raven dropped her chin and the rest of the tears fell onto her tightly twisted hands.

Tink groaned and threw back her chair, standing as tall as she could.

"We're holding you here. Let me know when you're ready to talk," she yelled, before marching out the room and slamming the door behind her.

Annie started to state the time and Tink's exit for the tape, ready to wrap things up, when Raven leant forward on her chair, elbows on the table.

"I know you're all worried about your colleague," she whispered. "And I know how it looks, I'm not stupid. Everything is pointing at me and at The Veiled Order, but if you want to see your friend again I am begging you to read the riddle."

"Why can't you just talk to me?" Annie said, exasperated. "Tell me what it is I need to know."

"The Veiled Order do not take kindly to those who speak freely outside of their circle. You of all people should know that."

"Why, why should I know that? Is that what happened to Mirage? He talked outside the circle."

Raven sat back heavily in her chair. Her whole body was trembling. Annie knew better than to push someone who was oscillating so wildly between angry and upset. Even though every bone in her body was screaming at her to shake the answers out of the woman, Annie bit her tongue and ended the conversation for the recording.

Tink was pacing the corridor, muttering under her breath like Muttley.

"Tink, you can stop now," Annie said, putting a hand on her shoulder as she passed.

Tink looked up at Annie, eyes focussing, face relaxing as though she'd forgotten Annie was there too.

"Sorry," said Tink. "Sorry, I'm just so worried about Swift and that little toe rag was too tight lipped for my liking. She knows something. Why won't she just tell us? I'm so angry right now I can't function."

Annie rubbed at Tink's arm, guiding her back through the corridors to the open plan office. The scent of stale coffee mixed with printer ink felt comforting as they sat down at their desks. Annie moved her mouse to bring her computer screen to life, the clock flashing a brain numbing three am.

"Swift is clever and strong and capable." Annie turned to look at Tink who hadn't moved from where she dropped into her chair. "He's been gone for roughly five hours, give or take. Officers are sweeping the theatre again and will let us know what they find. If Swift was here, what would he be telling us to do?"

"Go to bed," Tink snorted, looking at her desk as though it contained the answers.

"True," Annie laughed. "But he'd also be telling us to organise our thoughts and start this investigation. We know that Mirage was killed in the theatre, we know that the last place Swift was seen was in the theatre, so chances are the two are linked. So, let's stop worrying about what we can't fix or who won't talk, and concentrate on what we do know." Annie clicked her mouse and started skim reading her emails to see if there was anything of use. She hovered over a recently received one from Page and her heart skipped a beat. "And let's do that on the road."

"What? It's three in the morning. Where are we going?" The circles under Tink's eyes were deep and dark.

"Page has come through with Madame Seraphina's address, and I say we go pay her a visit."

THIRTEEN

ANNIE AND TINK SAT IN THE FRONT OF TINK'S
yellow Punto, the engine running, the heater blowing
warm air around them.

"Tell me again," Tink said, her hand hovering on
the key in the ignition.

"Sera Smith, otherwise known as Madame
Seraphina, was a regular visitor to my parents' home
when I was growing up. She knows all about me and
my past and Robins said I needed to be careful in case
she used it against me."

"Right," Tink nodded. "And how do you feel
about seeing her again?"

"Like I want to find Swift and I would gladly face
up to a Great White shark or an angry hippo in order
to get some answers about where he's gone."

Tink turned the key and the car fell silent.

"You know that Swift is likely to act like an angry

hippo when we find him if he knows you put yourself in danger to get him back."

Annie opened her door and stepped out into the relentless rain.

"I like to think of him more like a lion who's sometimes stepped on Lego." She slammed the door closed and winced as the loud bang echoed in the night.

"Of course you do." Tink shut her door and locked the car, and they stepped up to Madame Seraphina's front door.

Mim had been right about one thing. Madame Seraphina was doing alright for herself, and Annie guessed it wasn't by chance either. Her home was a great flint and brick barn conversion. Set alone in what Annie thought was at least a couple of acres, though it was hard to see in the dark. The brick weave driveway circled at the front of the building and a glass fronted section glistened in the moonlight.

"Being a cult leader pays well then?" Tink said, hammering at the door.

"She's never admitted to being a cult leader," Annie replied, pressing her hand up to the glass to peer in. "And I don't think we can call a magic circle a cult without getting sawn in half, but yeah, I guess it does."

The darkness beyond the glass was thick. Annie couldn't see past her own steamed up breath. There were no streetlights and no houses nearby to offer a subtle glow. The barn was almost triple height. The glass middle running from top to bottom was a pretty juxtaposition to the brick and flint that had had a facelift but was obviously the original. A property out this way, set alone with its own grounds and in-and-out driveways would have set Madame Seraphina back at least seven figures. Annie wiped at her breath on the glass with her sleeve and flinched as she came face to face with a woman she once knew well.

They appraised each other through the glass. Both older but recognisable. Annie only knew this as Madame Seraphina's face aged in the seconds it took her to place Annie. Her jaw dropped in a cliché of a move.

Tink held a hand up and Annie thought she was about to wave at the old woman through the glass, but instead she flashed her badge. Madame Seraphina's jaw dropped even further and she gathered her dressing gown around her chest and unlocked the door.

"Annie?" The older woman looked straight past the police badge. "Annie O'Malley is that really you? Is it Robert, has something happened to him? I have been waiting for this day for years ,but I never thought it would actually happen."

Madame Seraphina shrank under their gaze. Through the grey hair and the dressing gown, Annie could still see the young woman who'd filled their lives with Patchouli and pain. She started to reach out, wanting to touch Madame Seraphina's arm, to ground her in this new reality.

"DS Lock and Annie O'Malley," Tink interrupted the reunion and Annie drew her hand back. "We need to come in and talk to you about Gabriel Mirage."

Madame Seraphina gasped, choking on air and righting herself with a laugh.

"Not what I was expecting." She shook her head. "Annie, what do you have to do with *that man*?"

She spat out the words as though they were poison on her tongue and slowly drew her eyes back and forth between Tink's police badge and Annie. "Are you here in an official capacity too? Don't tell me you're following in the footsteps of your parents? I would have thought that they were enough to put anyone off."

Annie opened her mouth to protest that up until a few months ago she knew nothing about her parents both being in the police and certainly nothing to put her off a policing career, but remembered the sage words of Robins and closed it again quietly.

"Can we come in?" Tink asked again, stepping forward.

Madame Seraphina wasn't intimidated by the move. She sniffed, glancing again at the two women at her door in the middle of the night as if debating whether to shut it in their faces.

"Please?" Annie added, she needed to get in and talk to this woman.

Madame Seraphina dropped her shoulders and stepped back into the hallway to let Annie and Tink through the door, closing it softly behind them.

The barn conversion was every bit as grand on the inside as it had looked from the driveway. The double height ceilings held a wealth of beams, light wood set against the redness of the bricks and the blue of the flint. The staircase drifted up from the centre of the hallway and disappeared into the shadows of the gallery landing and behind the stairs was an open plan room stretching from the front to the back of the barn. The doors either side were closed off, but Annie could imagine cosy sitting rooms and an office with wall to ceiling bookshelves.

"You have a lovely home," said Annie, as she and Tink followed Madame Seraphina through to the back of the barn and an open plan kitchen.

She gestured for the two officers to sit up at the island and started filling a coffee machine with water and whole beans. The kitchen was aglow with low level lighting around the units and five ginormous but dim bulbs hanging down over the island. Annie felt like reaching up and pulling the end one, letting it go like a Newton's Cradle.

"Does magic really pay this well?" Tink asked, swiping her hands across the marble countertop.

Madame Seraphina ignored the question and worked her way around the kitchen, adding cream to a jug and crystallised sugar from a glass jar to a small ceramic sugar bowl. Placing a black coffee each in front of Annie and Tink, she cradled her own and stayed with the island as a barrier between her and the police.

"Gabriel Mirage, you say," said Madame Seraphina. "It's obviously something important to bring you out at such an hour, but I do have to warn you it's been a while since we spoke. How can I help you?"

"Madame Seraphina," Tink began.

"Please, call me Sera, I'm not at work right now," Madame Seraphina interrupted.

Annie's stomach twisted to hear her say her real name. As Madame Seraphina, Annie could almost disassociate this woman from the one who had been a part of her life growing up, but as Sera, Annie was thrown right back into it.

"Thank you, Sera," Tink continued. "We understand that you had some bad feelings between you, you and Gabriel."

"You could say that, why, what's he done?"

Sera was either a very good liar, or she had no idea of Gabriel's fate. And given how much she'd lied to the police back when Annie's dad had disappeared, Annie was hastened to think it was the former.

"Can you tell us a little about why you fell out of friendship?" It was Tink's turn to ignore the questions this time.

"Work stuff, nothing major."

"Can you explain this?" Tink pulled out her phone and turned it to Sara who held it up and away from her face, her eyes narrowing.

Magic obviously didn't help with poor eyesight.

"That's our website." Sera gave a non-answer.

120

"Okay, well we're detectives and funnily enough we had worked that out by ourselves. What we'd like to know is why Mirage has a large red cross through his face."

Annie was watching this all play out from the wings. Tink was a force of nature when she wanted something, and Annie was enjoying focussing on the body language of the two. Sera was a hard one to gauge; open arms and smile but hiding behind a slab of marble.

"The Veiled Order do not take kindly to being betrayed," said Sera, sipping her coffee. Steam rose around her face like a veil of smoke, lending her a gothic edge.

"Mirage betrayed you?" Tink asked. "How?"

Sera stepped back into the shadows, looking down at her drink.

"Not me," she said. "The Veiled Order."

"A group run by you, so we're led to believe," Tink replied. "Can you tell me more about the Order?"

Sera's eyes narrowed. "We're just a group of friends who all practice magic. Look, I don't mean to be rude, but you're asking me all these questions about my circle, and Mirage, and me and I still have no idea why you're here. To what end are all these questions?"

"Mirage was found dead during his magic show this evening." Tink didn't beat around the bush. Annie knew she wanted to see Sera's reaction and it was a clever way to do it. "Can you tell us where you were yesterday?"

But Sera was calm and collected and stayed for a beat in the shadows before taking a step forward and placing her cup down on the marble without a sound.

"I think I'd like to put pause to this conversation now, thank you," she said, her warmth had dropped a few degrees.

"You're refusing to answer any more questions? Refusing to tell us your alibi for the time of Mirage's death," Tink asked, cocking her head and radiating classic Tink friendliness.

"Not refusing, no," Sera replied, before turning to Annie. "But I have been in this situation before and had words put in my mouth. So if you need anything more from me then I will happily oblige at the station and in an environment where what I say can't be twisted."

Annie balked. Sera had been questioned time and time again by the police when Annie's dad had disappeared and she had twisted every single thing they said, been obtuse, and she'd blatantly lied to their faces. At least, that's what Annie had gathered from snippets of overheard conversations.

"Sera, please," Annie said, standing down from her high stool. "We have a colleague who's been taken, we don't know if he's safe and we need to find him. We're not here to twist your words, we're just here to find out what you know about the death of

Mirage and how it might be linked to Swift's disappearance."

"I'm sorry, Annie, I can't help you." Annie could feel the guilt radiating from Sera as she walked around the island and put her hand on the older woman's arm.

"Please." Annie' eyes were stinging with tears. "Swift... he means a lot to me as a friend, not just a colleague."

Sera placed a hand on Annie's and softly lifted it away from her arm, dropping it like a sack of rubbish.

"Your dad meant a lot to me and then poof, gone," she said, imitating a small explosion with her hands. "Have you thought that maybe this Swift person has left because he doesn't want to be found? That he's had enough and can't work up the courage to tell you, so leaving is easier."

It was like a punch to Annie's stomach. Sera wasn't talking about Swift, she was talking about Annie's dad.

"I'm sorry about what happened all those years ago, Sera," she said. "But this is not what's happening now. Mirage was murdered and our friend is missing and we're scared. All we're asking you to do is tell us what happened between the Veiled Order and Mirage and maybe we can figure out what's going on."

Sera leant into Annie's face, her breath hot with coffee.

"Your mum said the same thing to me when she came looking for Robert," she whispered. "And look what happened. I was harassed so much by the police that I had to leave the commune because I'd brought shame on them. I had no one, I was completely deserted by everyone I thought I could trust."

"My mum and dad?" Annie whispered back.

Sera shook her head.

"Your dad, yes," she said. "Your mum always hated me, probably for good reason. But no, I'm talking about the very people who had put me in that situation in the first place. My team. My work."

A sickening sense of realisation began to dawn on Annie. She gulped in air to stop herself from throwing up, feeling her skin mottle with sweat.

"You were working undercover too. With my parents."

"With your dad," she nodded. "He was my senior, supposed to watch out for me. In the end he left me, and then your mum ruined me."

Annie span around, the edges of her vision blurring with the movement. Out of the corner of her eye she saw Tink racing towards her.

"I'm okay," she said, righting herself. "I'm okay."

Tink stopped at Annie's side and nodded, drawing her shoulders back. Annie turned to Sera, studying the lines etched in her face, each line a year of a life that Annie needed to know more about. But she had to stop diving into the rabbit hole that was her past. Swift needed them and Annie needed Swift.

"I am *not* my parents," Annie said, drawing breath. "I am only a product of their neglect. So

124

please, if you have any sense of what's right, tell us what happened to Mirage."

It was the first time Annie had said out loud how she really felt about her childhood. Maybe the first time the realisation of how she had been treated had hit. There was a whole load of issues right there in that sentence that Annie needed to take to therapy, but for now, she needed to persuade Sera to talk. She only hoped it had been enough.

FOURTEEN

MADAME SERAPHINA MARCHED ACROSS THE ROOM, away from Annie and Tink and towards the glass wall that overlooked the back garden.

Annie had no idea of the time, but the sun had started to spread her fingers across the lawn, highlighting the mown stripes and the borders full of early blooming flowers. Sera ran her hands through her hair, grunting like she was toying with her good and bad sides. Devils and angels. A shoulder each, whispering into Sera's ears.

Tink looked at Annie. Mouthing *are you okay?* Annie nodded.

"Sorry," she whispered, keeping an eye on Sera from a distance. "I don't know what came over me. I need to focus on why we're here. Maybe Robins made a mistake adding me to this case."

Tink shook her head, tucking a strand of bleach

blonde hair behind her ear. She looked tired, tiny lines deepening under her eyes.

"Robins knows what she's doing," said Tink.

"Even if I have no idea," Annie sighed. "Do we press her for info?"

Tink drew her bottom lip between her teeth. Annie could see the doubt in her eyes. But before the young DS could answer, Sera slapped her hands against the glass with a bang.

"I may live to regret this," Sera said, her breath steaming up the wall. "But okay. I'll tell you what I know about Mirage."

When she turned to face the detectives, Sera's face had drained of colour so much it matched her hair. She looked older, tired, as though she wanted to be left alone.

"Gabriel Mirage is a great magician. *Was* a great magician."

Annie and Tink stepped up to where Sera was talking so she didn't have to raise her voice so much. They were in what looked like a formal living area, starched sofas and a coffee table with books at right angles.

"He had everything. The magic, the way with people, the glamour, the looks. Having your own theatre as a magician is a rarity, but Gabriel managed it well. I often wondered how he'd cope as a single parent with a young boy. Gabriel used to talk about Benjy's mum being a bit absent, but he'd never elaborate and then one day she vanished. Gabriel did everything for Benjy and they were like peas in a pod. Oh, poor Benjy, how is he?"

"He's being looked after," Tink said, softly.

Sera nodded. "Thank you." She took a deep breath. "We have a saying in the magic world that 'secrets are what create the mystery and without the secrets there is no magic.' Not very inventive, I suppose, but it's the stocks and shares of our work. If magicians started telling the world how we do our magic, then our livelihood would be taken away from us. The Veiled Order share magic amongst each other so we need to make sure we're all protecting that magic."

"What secrets did Mirage give away?" Tink asked.

"He lost his ethics for a girl." Sera shook her head as though love wasn't enough. "Mirage started acting all coy and giggly. He wouldn't tell us who the woman was, but he was being obvious enough that it was a woman. The texts, the dreamy looks, the happiness that comes with the lies of a new relationship."

"You think he spilled The Veiled Order secrets to whomever he was in love with?" Annie asked.

"I know he did," Sera replied. "He told me he had. He came to me all in a panic that he'd given away some secrets that he shouldn't have."

"And what did you do?" Tink asked.

The question hung in the air like a bad smell.

"I did what any leader would do," Sera replied, looking at the floor. "I held him accountable."

"You banished him from the group?" Annie asked.

Sera nodded, not looking quite so sure of her conviction now.

"Hence crossing out his name on the webpage?" Tink said.

"I had to make an example of him," Sera added, trying to convince someone; Annie wasn't sure it was just Sera herself.

"And how else did you do that?" Tink asked.

Sera pushed a bare toe into the deep pile of the rug she was standing on.

"I told the order he was banished, and that anyone caught talking to him would meet the same fate."

"So, you basically made Mirage a pariah?" Annie said.

"He did that to himself," Sera argued. "It wasn't my choice to have him spill our secrets."

"No, but it was your choice to treat him the way you did." Annie tried to look past the guilt in Sera's eyes, thinking about the way she'd treated her mum, she was nothing if not consistent. "Do you think there's anyone in the Veiled Order who would take what Mirage did to heart? Really have it out for him?"

Sera's eyes widened. "Kill him, you mean?"

"Yes," Tink replied.

"Not at all," Sera replied, incredulous. "There's no one like that."

"And did you find out who Mirage was in a relationship with?" Tink prompted when Sera added no more.

"He didn't say." Sera turned to look back out of the windowed wall. The garden was almost fully lit, surrounded by woodland and filled with colour it was tranquil and beautiful. "But if I was to hazard a guess, I'd be talking to that assistant of his."

"Candy?" Annie asked, surprised.

Candy was a teenager, and if spilling secrets wasn't a crime punishable by death in the eyes of the Veiled Order, then having an affair with a young girl definitely could be.

"I can't believe you didn't lamp her one," Tink said, as the two women pushed open the door to the incident room and bustled inside.

The sun had fully risen as they'd driven back across the countryside to the city headquarters. Annie's eyes felt gritty and sore, and she probably looked like the best friend of a drug baron. They'd left Sera with a card and the promise to call if she thought of anything else to tell them, but the magician had flagged after telling them her secrets and had taken herself up the grand staircase to lie down.

"When she talked about Mum and Dad?" Annie asked, twisting the cord on the blinds and flooding the room with sunshine. "There's so much I don't know, Tink. So much that I can't even begin to piece together. But Swift is my priority, and if I'd knocked Sera on the chin with my fists, she'd not have told us about Mirage and Candy. What do you make of that?"

Tink picked up a pen and started writing on the whiteboard. She circled Mirage's name in the middle of the board and jotted down the details that Sera had given them underneath.

"So, we've got Gabriel Mirage, otherwise known as Keith Stuckley. Great magician, great dad, great person all round, except for the fact he might be in a relationship with a minor. Found dead in his vanishing cabinet, murdered by all accounts with a gas chamber full of Carbon Monoxide. We might have a couple of motives now. One, he gave away magic secrets; flimsy at best. Two, his new relationship; more likely to be a reason to want to hurt him."

"We're not sure Candy is actually a minor, she might be over sixteen for all we know." Annie scrunched up her nose.

"We need to find out, but even if she's eighteen, Mirage was in his late thirties and in a position of power. It's still not sitting right with me."

"Yeah, even as I said that it felt wrong." Annie nodded for Tink to continue.

"Alongside Mirage we have his old magic circle, The Veiled Order, who threw him out for telling secrets." Tink tapped her pen under where she'd written the Order before writing Madame Seraphina and circling it frantically. "And Seraphina is still a suspect, no matter how well she hid it. She pitted the Order against Mirage, and she has a past history of being evasive. She would know how the vanishing cabinet worked and be able to rig up something like the Carbon Monoxide contraption we found, given her previous life working in a self-sufficient commune. She also avoided giving us an alibi for the time of Mirage's murder. It's not quite enough to bring her in on charges, but we can try and get her in to make a statement, press her for more details."

Annie nodded.

"And Raven whose riddle we still need to go over." Tink blew out air and added Raven's name to the mix. "She was seen in the theatre at the time of Mirage's death, could well be pissed at him for giving away her secrets. We know they didn't like each other and that Benjy was warned to stay away from her and tell his dad if she ever came by their place. Why would he have done that if he wasn't a bit scared of what she could do?"

Surrounding Mirage's name on the whiteboard was Madame Seraphina, Candy, and Raven, and Annie had an itch she couldn't scratch that they were missing an important name on that board. They were all possible suspects with credible motives, but something wasn't sitting right with her, and she couldn't work out what.

"Swift," she shouted, making Tink jump so hard she dropped the pen. "Sorry, sorry, I just…"

"Okay," Tink said, picking the pen off the floor

and adding Swift's name to the left of the others. "Tell me again what happened."

Annie chewed at her lip, closing her eyes and putting herself back in the depths of the theatre belly.

"We were thinking about how Candy climbed in to the theatre through a window because she didn't have keys to the main door," she started. "How that would be a fire hazard if there was only one main entrance and one fire door that didn't look as though it had ever been used. Then Swift talked about how his school had stages like the one in the theatre and we went to look at it and I felt a breeze at my feet that made me think there was a window or a door nearby. We found the trapdoor and down under the theatre was like a storage unit filled to the brim with Mirage's old crap."

"And another door?" Tink asked, twisting the pen around her fingers.

"And another door." Annie nodded, picturing the way the door had a clear path to it and swung open easily. "It led up to the far outside of the pier and down to the water."

"But Swift didn't go that way?"

"No, in fact, Swift didn't even get to the door to see it before he had to excuse himself because he was having a coughing fit." Annie toyed with what Sera had said back at the barn. "Tink, do you think Swift used his coughing fit as an excuse to leave me down there?"

"Not even for a second, Annie," Tink said,

shaking the pen at O'Malley. "And don't you let that woman make you think so. There's a world of a difference between what's going on with you and Swift and the shit that was going on between your parents. Swift would never, ever leave his team or you in the lurch like this."

"Even if I thought we were going on a date last night and it turns out it was a team outing?" Annie felt her cheeks heat. "What if I made it obvious that's what I thought and then Swift vanished because he couldn't handle the pressure from me?"

"Stop right there, missus," Tink said, hands on hips. Annie could see where the unlidded pen was starting to mark Tink's top but when she opened her mouth to let Tink know she was shut down immediately. "Swift wanted to go on a date with you too, but he thought it would be too much for you, which is why Page and I were tagging along. No. Swift did not leave because of you, and may I suggest politely that when he's back you two sit down and have a proper conversation?"

Annie nodded, her eyes spilling with tears.

"Tink, what if he doesn't come back? What if we never find him. There was someone in that cabinet when I came out from under the stage and when I looked it was empty."

"People don't just disappear, Annie," Tink said.

But Annie had first-hand experience of just that, and her sister hadn't reappeared for over fifteen years.

"Then where is he? What happened to him in the time it took me to notice he was gone?"

Tink looked at her hands, noticing the pen marks. "We need to check with Robins to see if there's been any contact."

The door to the incident room swung open with a bang and both women jumped, their heads spinning in the direction of the doorway. Page and Robins stood there with faces so grim that Annie's stomach dropped all the way to her toes.

FIFTEEN

It felt like it took a whole millennium for Robins to usher Page inside and shut the door gently behind them. All the while Annie was waiting for Robins to tell them they'd found Swift and that it wasn't good news. It was written all over her face.

Annie couldn't take it; she felt her chest constrict so hard her breath stopped at the base of her tongue. She gripped at the edge of the table and sat with a thump on the chair, gasping for air.

"Breathe Annie," Tink said, rubbing her back with hands so sweaty they were sticking to Annie's top. "It's going to be okay. Isn't it?"

Tink aimed that at Robins who had taken herself to the front of the room and was studying the board. She turned to face the present members of the MCU and cleared her throat.

"I've got some news," she said, her voice shaky. "Officers have spent the last few hours searching for signs of Swift or evidence of if and where he has been taken. There was nothing on the stage, backstage, or up in the flat that gave us any clue as to what has happened to the DI."

"What are you not telling us?" Annie shouted, half out of her chair. "Please, Robins. What have you found."

Robins opened her coat and drew out what looked like a sealed evidence bag. She held it up to the team and Annie cried out.

"Do any of you recognise this?" she asked.

Annie would recognise Swift's phone anywhere. From the crack in the screen to the ill-fitting case, the old iPhone that was normally glued to the DI was swinging from Robins' hands in a bag that meant the worst.

"Where did you find it?" Annie asked, trying to regulate her breathing.

"It was in the vanishing cabinet," Robins said, putting the evidence on the table. "In the secret compartment."

"The secret compartment was open," Annie blurted. "Maybe he dropped it when he was taken."

Annie could have sworn she'd looked for any traces of Swift in the cabinet when she realised he'd gone missing, but she could have passed over a small phone in her panic.

"No, the door to the secret compartment was shut when officers looked," Robins said. "They used your notes to open it, reported that the phone looked like it had been dropped there."

"The secret compartment was shut?" Annie's head swam.

"Yes."

"But that's not right," Annie cried. "That compartment was open when I looked in there. Who shut it? Why did they shut it? There's no way his phone could have gotten in there without him, is there? There's no way that Swift could have been hiding in there when I looked because I swear it was all open. Why would they take him back in there rather than outside? Why would they hide him in there?"

Annie was answering all of her own questions in her mind with the bleakest of solutions. They did to Swift what they did to Mirage. They had been hiding in the building the whole time and Swift had come across them, so they had to take him out too.

"We've organised for divers to search along the coastline by the pier at first light," Robins said, grimly matching Annie's thoughts.

The room fell silent, pulsing with all the unasked questions and trapped emotions. Annie felt like she was drowning, like she too had been thrown into the choppy waters under the pier and couldn't surface. The lights around her were fading into blackness and she wanted to accept the fate and lay her head on the desk and never wake up. Annie spread her arms on the cool tabletop and burrowed her head in their safety.

If I were you, I'd rehash the evidence. Go over what you haven't given enough time to yet.

Swift's methodical voice was like an ear worm. There's no way he would give up like this if it was a member of his team who had gone. He would work and rework and scratch through the evidence until his fingers were bleeding before he lay his head in defeat.

"This is not my past repeating itself," Annie muffled into the crooks of her elbows. "The divers won't find him because he's not in the sea. Why would he be in the sea? There's no reason for the person who killed Mirage to kill Swift too." There were a million and one reasons, but Annie was choosing to ignore them. "Tink, where's the riddle that Raven left us? We need to go over it again, line by line, word by word. There's something there I didn't see the first time around. I think it's more than just a distraction."

"It's in evidence," Tink replied. "Forensics are trying to find anything they can on it."

Annie nodded, drawing her phone from her pocket. "Okay, well in that case I'll write it out on the board and we can look at it anew."

She opened her photos and rose from her chair, taking the pen that Tink had been gripping in her hands and walking to the whiteboard.

In a theatre filled with wonder, where illusions come to life,

A magician's grand performance, causing
wonder and strife.
After the cheers have fallen, a disappearance takes its toll,
A missing person vanishes, not the magician's control.

Through trapdoors and secret panels,
the magician cast their spell,
But when the curtains part once more,
the mystery deepens, oh so well.
With robes of velvet, wands in hand,
they vanish into air,
Leaving behind a mystery, a puzzle oh so
rare.

So tell me, dear seeker, with your keen
and watchful eye,
Where did the magic lead them? Solve
this riddle, I do not lie.
For in the heart of wizardry, where
dreams and spells entwine,
The missing person waits for you, their
fate within your mind.

She tapped her pen against the first line, all eyes
on Annie.

"Okay, so we have the theatre and Mirage's
performance causing wonder, which it did, and strife,

when he was found dead?" Annie said, looking for some nod to keep going from her team.

Page looked like he was surviving on adrenaline and caffeine, his pale face and sunken eyes a give-away that he wasn't as chirpy as normal. His shirt was crumpled, designed for a night at the theatre, not a night solving the worst crime possible. Annie looked at Tink and then down at the jeans and jumper she'd borrowed from Swift and realised they all looked like they'd been on the tiles and come into work straight from their night out. Only Robins was dressed in her usual work wear of a tailored suit, but even she looked displaced with hair untucked from its bob and lack of bright lipstick. But all eyes were on Annie like she had the answers, so she continued, unsure of where she was going.

"And then after the performance someone goes missing, but it's beyond the magician's control," Annie said, slowly, trying to piece the puzzle with real life. "But we know it's not in his control because he's dead, right?"

The team nodded at her.

"So which magician is it talking about? Seraphina? The Veiled Order? Raven?" Annie threw her hands up in frustration. "Why didn't Raven just write in clear, precise words what happened to Swift?"

"Keep going," Page said, head resting on his palms. "There's got to be something here."

"Okay, okay," Annie turned back. "Trapdoors and

secret panels; the stage and the cabinet? Curtains, mystery, wands, all an illusion maybe? A rare puzzle. What's the rarest puzzle, or the hardest to work out puzzle in magic?"

Annie flung her head around and looked at her team. They shook their heads back, shrugging.

"Work it out. We need to work it out. Because I think this is where the magic leads us and where Swift is. Look, the missing person waits for us." Annie tapped her pen so hard on the whiteboard over the word *waits* that ink flew all over her hands. "Swift isn't dead, he's waiting for us somewhere in a rare puzzle."

Annie wiped her mouth with the back of her hand, realising how parched she was. The cogs were turning in her mind, not quite aligning yet, but Annie knew there was something in the riddle. It wasn't just a random rhyme designed to throw them off course, it was a key to what had happened. But the faces of the rest of the MCU told her otherwise.

"Annie, come and sit down." Robins got up and pulled her chair out for Annie. "I do understand where you're coming from, we all want Swift to be okay, but we have to be realistic. This riddle could be interpreted in many different ways and I think that's what Raven wanted us to waste time doing. Maybe while she was planting this, Swift was being moved while we were all distracted with something pointing us in the wrong direction."

"Swift was being moved?" Annie said, brow

furrowed. She hadn't gone to sit down, nor did she want to. There was too much nervous energy whirling around her body to sit down. "Swift would lash out if he was being moved, he'd find a way to let us know. There's no way he'd take being moved lying down."

Robins looked at the table, face drawn. Annie had a sickening realisation that Swift being moved wasn't Swift, it was his body.

"You think the Order wanted to distract us with this riddle so they could take Swift's body down under the stage and throw it in the sea, don't you?" said Annie; her face felt hot. "Why though? Why did the Order kill Swift?"

"Because they killed Mirage and Swift worked out how," Robins answered as though she'd decided this fate back when Swift went missing.

Annie thought back to their meeting with Sera. "But the leader of the Order seemed genuinely shocked when we said Mirage had died, let alone one of our own going missing."

"She's pulled the wool over the eyes of the police before, Annie," Robins said. "Let's not let her do it again, hey?"

"No," Annie slammed her palms down on the table, sending the pen flying. "No. Don't make out that I can't see something when it's right in front of my own face. You hired me for my ability to see past the facade and that's what I'm doing. Swift is out there and he needs us."

Robins gaze hooked on Annie's, not letting go.

She held it for a beat too long and then walked to the door.

"I didn't hire you, Annie," she said, letting herself out of the room. "Swift did."

Annie felt like she'd been punched in the stomach.

"What does that mean?" she asked Tink and Page who looked as sick as she felt. "What does that even mean?"

"I think Robins is feeling as distraught as the rest of us," Page offered. "Please don't take it to heart. You're right, O'Malley, you do see things when the rest of us are oblivious."

"So you both agree with me then?" Annie pleaded. "Swift is okay."

Neither Tink nor Page spoke. The room dropped in volume again, plunging Annie even further.

"Great. Thanks guys." Annie grabbed her coat and marched to the door, flinging it open with such force that it bashed painfully on her shoulder and back into the face of a uniformed officer whose hand was raised ready to knock. "What?"

Annie's shout made the uniform take a step back. He held out a piece of paper with some figures on it and Annie snatched it from his hand. She glanced over the data, not quite able to focus on what she was reading. She looked up at the officer, brows raised.

"Yes?"

"Fingerprints lifted from the fire cracker packet

found in the theatre bin," the man said, taking another step back. "They're Candy's."

SIXTEEN

CANDY WASN'T AT HOME. HER MUM ANSWERED THE
door in a dressing gown looking like a child herself
with make-up free clear skin and her hair bundled on
top of her head. They lived in a neat semi in the
village of Wexwade with a friendly spaniel and an
array of pot plants lining the front path.

"May we come in for a moment please, Mrs
Atherton?" Annie asked, smiling even though it was
hurting her face using muscles that didn't want to
work.

"Miss, but please call me Claire. Is everything
okay?" Miss Atherton stepped back and left room for
Tink and Annie to pass by her into the tidy living
room.

Page had been given a few hours leave to go and
check on his gran and let the carer know what was
going on. Annie felt for him, not only did he have
work to think about, he also had his gran at home to

look after. Annie only had Sunday the cat and a pot plant, and she couldn't remember when she last fed either of them. She'd typed out a quick message to Pete the pizza man who owned the eatery under her flat and asked him to check in on the cat to make sure he was okay. Pete had replied almost immediately to let Annie know that Sunday had been asleep in the window of the Pizza Parlour all night with a belly full of BBQ chicken.

"We're actually looking for Candy, if she's around?" Tink replied, perching on the edge of a floral sofa. "We'd like to have a chat with her about Mirage, Keith."

Annie sat next to Tink and Claire sat on an upright armchair opposite, the spaniel lying down at her feet and looking up at her with big brown eyes. The room was bright and airy and clean, photos lined the walls along with bright artwork and the tv was small and tucked away in a corner.

Claire shook her head. "She's with Benjy still, popped back home for a quick shower and a change of clothes but she wanted to stay with the little boy and make sure he was okay. Such sad news, Keith was a good man. Do you know what happened?"

"Did Candy get on well with Keith?" Annie asked. "When we saw her in the theatre before the show, she seemed to be enjoying her job, but she looked like she was worked quite hard. How did that feel to her? Was there any reason she took on such a large role at such a young age?"

Claire smiled a knowing smile. "Candy has always been a bit of a force of nature. She's only sixteen but you'd never know it."

Annie could feel Tink's bubbling anger brewing beside her, but she stayed outwardly cool.

"She certainly acts older," Tink added.

"It's always just been the two of us so I guess she had my attention to herself and we learnt and grew together," Claire replied. "We'd take walks along the pier as soon as she was able to toddle about. She loves it there. So when Keith said he was looking for an assistant to help him in the theatre, Candy jumped at the chance, even though she was only fourteen at the time."

"And Keith was okay with hiring a minor?" Tink asked.

"Oh yes," Claire laughed ironically. "He liked the idea of a lesser wage. But they got on like a house on fire and soon Candy was working all hours she had free. I make sure she does her homework first, of course, but she's learning the magical ropes from Keith. Oh... I mean she was learning the ropes. Oh goodness, poor Candy will be bereft when it hits her."

Claire's hand covered her lips, her fingers shaking.

"Did you ever get the sense that there was more to the theatre than Candy said?" Annie asked.

"What do you mean?" Claire's eyes narrowed.

"Between Candy and Keith."

"Oh Lordy, never," Claire laughed again. "Candy

enjoyed the company of an adult male, I suppose, seeing as there is a lack of one at home." She opened her arms, gesturing to the very feminine surroundings. Annie felt a chill finger its way up her spine. "But they worked well together, had a laugh together, and they always got on, even when Candy was moaning about how he was always late."

"And did they spend time together outside of work?" Tink asked.

"Of course," Claire replied, and Annie could see cogs whirring in Claire's mind. "Keith was teaching Candy, she would pop over after school when she didn't have clubs. She'd always come home exhilarated and full of talk."

Annie and Tink stayed quiet.

"Look, I know what you're getting at, but no, there was nothing untoward going on between my daughter and Keith," Claire said, pointedly, though Annie could hear the lilt of apprehension in her words.

"You said Candy is with Benjy now?" Annie tried a new tact. "Does she have a good friendship with the boy?"

"I think growing up in a single parent family, Candy knows what it's like for Benjy when he's kept out of the loop on show nights. She likes to make sure he's okay and safe." Tears sprang into Claire's eyes, and she blinked them down her cheeks, wiping them with the sleeve of her dressing gown. "What will happen to him? Will Candy still be able to see him?"

"We hope so, yes," Annie answered. "But truly it depends on what his mum decides to do. We hope that she will always facilitate the relationship between the two children, given how close they are."

Claire hummed sadly. "Keith said she never wanted anything to do with Benjy, it all seems so unfair that she now has custody and Keith is lying cold in the ground."

He wasn't quite yet, Mirage wouldn't be buried until they worked out what had happened to him and who had happened to him, but Annie didn't correct Candy's mum.

"Is it okay if we talk to Candy at Benjy's mum's house, or would you like to be present?" Annie asked.

"You can talk to her about last night, that's fine, but if you want to talk about more than that, I'd like to be there please." Claire nibbled on her fingernails.

"We'll see what Candy says," Tink added. "Is Benjy's mum nearby, do you know?"

"Zoe Stuckley went away for a while when she split from Keith, but she came back recently and looks amazing. She lives in the posh part though, on the other side. Large house all out on its own, you can't miss it."

CANDY'S MUM WAS RIGHT. THIS WASN'T A BLINK AND you miss it property, it was huge. Annie and Tink looked at it from the car, straining their necks to see the pitched roof atop the Georgian pile.

"What do you think?" Annie asked Tink as she turned the key and the engine clicked off.

"I think I'd like to know what Mrs Stuckley does that pays this well, because it's certainly not police work." Tink whistled through her teeth.

"About Candy and Mirage you twit." Annie nudged the DS with a soft elbow.

"Oh, right." Tink sat back. "Well I think there was something between the two of them and I think it might have gotten Mirage killed. Candy is sixteen. She was working overtime and spending lots of hours with this guy. He was in a new relationship and a happy bunny. Sixteen, Annie, urgh."

"Fourteen when she started working with him," Annie reminded her colleague.

"Do you think he was waiting until she was a bit older before he started anything?"

"Grooming her, you mean?"

"Yeah," Tink sighed. "Grooming her. What a world we live in."

"Do you think the Order found out? Maybe he wasn't banished because he was giving away secrets, maybe he was banished because of Candy. And Sera didn't tell us because that's an obvious motive to kill him before he brings down The Veiled Order's name."

"I think you've hit the nail on the head there, O'Malley." Tink opened her door. "Come on, let's see what Candy has to say for herself. Because she was most likely the one who bought those firecrackers and my guess is she used them too."

"So maybe it wasn't the Order who set Mirage up to die, maybe Candy had been used enough?" Annie shut her door behind her.

Tink nodded and Annie followed her to the front door of Mrs Stuckley's home and listened as the bell chimed loudly. There was a piece of the puzzle that wasn't quite working for Annie and she couldn't put her finger on it. But there was no time to figure it through as the door was pulled open and a smart looking woman with a high ponytail and athleisurewear stood there staring at them.

"Yes?" she said, hands on her tiny hips. "Can I help you? I'm extremely busy right now so I don't want to buy anything or hear about a god I don't worship or listen to how you've just got out of prison and need to sell me dishcloths to get in your probation officers' good books."

She poked out a hip and stared at the women, waiting for an answer. Annie puffed out her cheeks, she knew she looked bad given what she was wearing and she hadn't brushed her hair or her teeth for longer than she'd like to remember, but that was a low blow. Tink was unfazed as she pulled out her card.

"Police," she said, stonily. "We'd like to come in and talk to you about Keith Stuckley and we're also here to see Candy Atherton. Can we come in?"

Zoe Stuckley's eyes widened.

"Oh goodness me, sorry," she laughed. "We get a

lot of cold callers here, they think we have money. We do, but I'm not going to be giving it to any Tom, Dick, or Harry, am I? Please come in."

Annie and Tink wiped their feet and Annie noticed Tink checking her phone, swiping through emails not as discretely as normal.

"Anything?" she whispered, as they followed Zoe Stuckley through a cavernous hallway to a small snug off the kitchen.

"I'll be right back," Zoe said, disappearing back out the way they came.

Annie looked at her watch. It was late enough and light enough that the divers would be out. Annie figured if they found anything that Robins would call them, but she also didn't want to look at her phone in case she had any missed calls. Swift was going to be okay; it was her mantra and Annie was sticking to it.

"Nothing yet," Tink replied quietly, engrossed in something on her screen. "Though the tech team have started going through the paperwork you found under the stage and forensics are having a field day with the samples from the vanishing cabinet. Apparently, there's a lot of bodily fluid in the secret compartment."

"What?" Annie hissed. "From Mirage?"

"They're testing DNA now but they want us to go back to the theatre when we're done here."

"I need to pick up my car anyway." Annie nodded as Zoe appeared back in the room with an oversized sweater over her vest top and leggings.

"Sorry about that, I was just checking on Benjy and Candy." Zoe leant against the windowsill, the sun illuminating her like a halo.

"How are they? It can't be easy for either of them." Annie was taking in Zoe, she looked young, too young to have a small child. She wondered if that was the reason for Mirage having custody of Benjy. Something inside her shifted, unsettling her.

"They're okay," Zoe replied, cheerily. "They're playing on the PS5, Candy is so good with him, isn't she, like a little mum herself? She'll be a godsend when I have to go back to work on Monday. Promised me she'll come and look after him."

"Doesn't Candy have school?" Tink asked.

"Oh, haha, it's the Easter holidays," Zoe's cheeks flushed a pretty pink. "Of course she'll prioritise school."

Annie smiled back at Zoe. "Can you tell us a little about your relationship with Mirage? With Keith, sorry. And I am sorry for your loss."

Something flashed in Zoe's eyes, but she caught it before it spilled out of her lips.

"Keith and I met when I was just leaving high school. He was a few years older than me and I liked the attention he gave me."

"Where did you meet?" Annie asked.

"The theatre, though Wexwade is small so we kind of knew each other anyway. I used to hang out on the pier as a teen, like most of the teens in this town. We'd drink and smoke, like. It's known as the place to be."

"And can you tell us what happened between you?" Tink said, settling back on the sofa.

"We grew apart when Benjy came along. I think that Keith had longed for a child for so long that he completely smothered Benjy in love and neglected me."

"And did you not mind that he had full custody of your child?" Tink probed.

There was the flash again, darting in and out of Zoe's eyes like a snake's tongue. She pushed away from the window and opened the snug door, calling out for Candy.

"What could I do?" she asked, turning back to the officers. "I was young, I still wanted to go out and behave like a girl in my twenties. It was for the best. I couldn't be a mum; I couldn't protect Benjy."

Annie's mind whirred, *protect Benjy from what?*

SEVENTEEN

WHEN CANDY DIDN'T MAKE AN APPEARANCE, ZOE called out for her again, this time leaving the room.

"Protect Benjy?" Tink whispered when they were alone.

"My first thought too." Annie span around and looked at Tink. "Mirage had a relationship with Zoe when she was young."

"And vulnerable," Tink interrupted. "I've seen the state of the kids that hang out on Wexwade pier and let me tell you they are not the kind of kids whose parents give them milk and cookies after school and sit down at a table to eat dinner. Zoe could have been one of them, she could have been prey for a man like Mirage."

"Wow, right okay." Annie tapped at her lips with her forefingers. "So Zoe and Candy, I'm sensing a theme. So why did Zoe say she couldn't protect

Benjy? Benjy is Mirage's son so surely...? It's all getting a little morbid."

"Feel like I'm going to throw up a little in my mouth."

Tink held out her hand and Annie gripped it, their palms both slick.

"Let's see if we can get Candy to talk." The door opened, interrupting Tink. Candy walked through. She was on her own, half in half out the room, eyes darting back out to where she'd come from.

"Come in Candy, we've spoken to your mum and she said it's okay for us to talk to you about last night," Annie said, trying to make the girl feel welcome. "But we're happy to take you home now and we can talk there if you'd rather? With your mum present."

"No!" Candy looked at them, with one foot still holding the door open. "Please, let's just talk here."

"How are you, Candy?" Annie asked.

"How do you think?" Candy spat. "Keith's dead and I'm here and nobody cares about how I feel."

"How do you feel?" Tink said, softly.

"Like I want to cry." Candy's lip wobbled. "I can't talk to mum about it because she'll be mad at me and I can't talk to you guys because you're going to go all official on me. I'm scared."

"What's scaring you?" Annie asked, gesturing for Candy to sit with them.

Candy shook her head, glancing again out of the door.

"I can't tell *you*, can I?" She was defiant in the way teenagers often were, with a little sass and a lot of fear.

Annie glanced across at Tink who gave a subtle nod of encouragement. This was Annie's forte, getting people to talk truthfully. But Annie was feeling the pressure, and that mixed with the lack of confidence in her from Robins was wearing her down.

"Candy, you can be honest with us, we're here to help you," she started. "Nothing else."

"No," Candy jutted her chin at Annie. "You're here to do anything in your power to find your friend. That's what I've heard. You'll take down anyone so long as you get him."

Tink's brow scrunched. "Heard from who?"

"Of course we're worried about DI Swift," Annie said, her voice thick. She cleared her throat. "But we're not here about him. We're here about Mirage. Candy, we know you bought the firecrackers, your fingerprints are on them."

"Yeah, I buy them for Benjy, he likes the noise they make. Why? You told me you only took my prints to eliminate them from the scene," Candy spat.

"We did," Annie went on. "But when they were found on the packet of firecrackers in the theatre bin, of course we need to ask about them. Look, do you think it would be better to do this at the station where you might feel more at ease?"

Candy barked out a laugh. "Oh yeah, here we go. Lull me in and then drag me down the station. You're not taking me anywhere. And what have the fire-crackers got to do with anything?"

Annie held her hands up in defeat. "Okay, Candy, we're not trying to trick you. We honestly just want to help. If you were just protecting yourself, you can tell us, you know. The police aren't bad people, we're not all the things you read about or watch on tv."

The young girl peered around the door to Annie and Tink. She looked like a child standing there in joggers and a jumper two sizes too big and quite obviously borrowed from Zoe Stuckley.

"But you need to tell us the truth for us to be able to protect you," Tink added.

"Protect me. You think you can protect me? What kind of protection did you offer him, hey?" Candy eyed them both, a steely gaze that cut through the silence that her words had left. She gave an angry grunt and marched out the room, slamming the door behind her.

"That went well," Annie said, sighing. "She's scared but she knows something. I think she's lying about the firecrackers, there was no other evidence in the flat that they'd been bought or played with previously. And what do you think she meant by we didn't protect him?"

Tink stood and walked to the window, looking out over the dew-covered grass.

"I wonder if Candy had feelings for Mirage," said Tink. "If she was so brainwashed that she actually thought she loved him?"

Annie tapped her fingers on her knee, looking at Tink and the grass beyond the window. The sun was streaming through the clouds, burning off the last of the rain and teasing to be a glorious day. But all Annie could think about was how much easier it would be for the divers to see if it wasn't raining.

"I'm not sure," she replied, realising Tink was waiting for her to speak. "There's something troubling me about this whole situation, I feel like we've got separate things going on and maybe we're confusing them."

"What do you mean? Mirage is dead and Swift is missing and they're very much connected."

Annie ran a hand through her hair, pulling it up and tying it with the hairband that had been cutting off the circulation on her wrist.

"Yeah, they are. Swift went missing in the theatre where Mirage was killed, they're most likely connected. But I meant that we have the two angles of The Veiled Order and the other people in Mirage's life."

Annie held out a hand for each one, weighing them up.

"And you think they're the ones that aren't connected?" Tink leant against the windowsill, her head cocked.

"I don't know what I think anymore, I normally run my crazy ideas past Swift and he moulds them into something reasonable." Annie looked down at her hands.

"I know," Tink said. "I miss him too. He's like a surrogate older brother to me, though don't tell him I said that. He's looked out for me since I joined the force, took me under his wing, though I have no idea why."

"He's a nurturer," Annie offered. "And he once told me that he saw potential in you and wanted to selfishly keep that for his own team."

Tink laughed. "Sounds about right."

They fell quiet, both thinking their own thoughts about their DI. A clock ticked somewhere in the house. A bird cried outside the window. It was peaceful, outwardly, but Annie's head was screaming with *what ifs*.

"I'm glad he did," Tink said eventually.

"Me too," Annie replied, softly. "I'm glad he got the opportunity to mentor you, you're an asset to our team, Tink. And think, if Joe hadn't got his claws in, you might have had to work your way through Traffic to get to CID."

Tink laughed again, a giggle that made Annie smile in return. Deep inside her mind there was a seedling of thought that Annie knew was growing into something important. She ignored it as best she could, knowing that if she forced it, she'd lead it on the wrong path.

"No thanks," she replied. "I'd rather stay on the beat than work Traffic, yawn. Imagine me in Traffic."

"You drive fast enough," Annie added with a smile.

"Ha ha," Tink said, pushing off from the window and opening the door a fraction. "I learn from the best."

Annie knew she was talking about Swift and her heart ached.

"Listen," Tink said, putting her ear to the crack in the door.

"What, I can't hear anything," Annie said, trying to hear what Tink was talking about over the song of the birds through the sash window.

"Exactly," Tink nodded. "Where is everyone? What's happened to Candy and Benjy, because I may not know a lot about children, but I know they're very rarely quiet when they're awake."

Tink drew back into the room.

"It's a big house," Annie said. "They might be right at the other side."

"I don't know, it feels off."

"You think Benjy is in danger around Candy?" Annie asked, wondering at the way Candy had been round the young boy. She'd stopped at nothing to be with him and stay with him.

Tink's brow pinched, and she set her hazel eyes on Annie, concern rippling through them. "Maybe Benjy reminds Candy of Mirage."

"Of course Benjy reminds her of Keith." Zoe poked her head around the door. "He's the spit of his dad. Always was."

Annie stood from the sofa and brushed down her

jeans. They felt loose against her legs because they were meant for Swift.

"Zoe, do you know if Mirage had found himself in a new relationship recently? Started seeing someone on the quiet, maybe, or keeping it a secret as it was new." Annie stepped aside to let Zoe past. The young mum dropped to the sofa, taking up the place Annie had just vacated.

"I'd heard rumours that was the case, yes," Zoe said, sitting poised and ready for something. "I recognised it in him too, he always held himself a few inches taller when he had the support of a woman."

Tink rounded the other side of the sofa so the detectives were flanking the woman, standing over her, trying not to appear too intimidating.

"Zoe, we have reason to believe we know who this person was," Tink said, choosing her words carefully. "Do you know? Would you be in a position to confirm our suspicions?"

Zoe nodded, heavy browed. "I may not have been able to spend time with Benjy but I still cared about him, I needed to know if Keith was introducing him to new people. I made sure I kept up to date with the comings and goings around the theatre."

Annie sat down next to Zoe, their knees almost touching.

"Zoe, were Mirage and Candy in a relationship?" she said, watching the woman's face for signs that the conversation was too much.

But Zoe's face was not quite moving how Annie had expected. First she tilted her head one way, her brows together. Then she tilted it the other way, confusion still rife. Her mouth opened and closed; no words expelled. She looked like a goldfish. Annie's brain was whirring.

"I'm sorry, what?" Zoe spluttered, eventually getting her words out, the corners of her mouth lifting. "You think that Keith... and Candy? Candy who is a child. Keith who definitely wasn't a child. Oh goodness me, you two crack me up. Call yourselves detectives."

Zoe slapped a hand against her knee like they were in a tv sitcom. Annie felt blood rush to her cheeks. Had they got this wrong?

"We thought that Mirage liked his companions to be on the younger side. There's you and Candy," Tink said, trying to justify their questions.

Zoe laughed so loudly it made Annie jump.

"Keith wasn't a nonce," Zoe said, her posh accent slipping ever so slightly. "Keith and me were in love and it was consensual. I was almost twenty when we got together. Keith was a little older but not that old. And Candy? Do me a favour, there is absolutely no way in this world that Keith would have even looked at her. Candy. Ha."

Zoe may have been laughing at the idea of Candy and Mirage being together but then who was Mirage in a new relationship with and why did it matter so much to their investigation?

"Zoe." Annie stopped her. "Okay, so we've got

164

that wrong, but someone out there still killed Mirage and if it's not to do with his predilection to young girls then we need to rethink and we need to do it fast."

Zoe looked taken aback. "Keith wasn't killed because he liked young girls, because Keith *didn't like* young girls. He had normal tastes just like you or I. If you have normal tastes. I'm guessing you do, given how worried you look that your colleague is missing. My guess is your tastes run to the DI. Very sad what happened to him."

What. Annie didn't have time to unpick how it was that everyone who came across her and Swift could see how they felt about each other, except each other. She needed answers.

"So who was he in a relationship with?" she pressed. "And why was he keeping it secret?"

Zoe's mouth drew into a smile that didn't reach her eyes. "Keith was in a relationship with Isabelle Raven."

EIGHTEEN

"Shite, shite, shite." Annie was holding on to the handle above the passenger car door as Tink drove like a madwoman across Wexwade to the theatre. "She has pulled the wool over all of our eyes. Was it Raven who pointed us in the wrong direction. Did she put the idea of Candy in our minds? The idea of Mirage being out to hurt young girls."

Tink hit the horn at a BMW driver who was trying to overtake the cars in front of them. He swerved back into his place and Tink overtook them instead. Annie would have apologised to the guy sticking his finger up at them had it not been for the fact she'd been dangerously tailgated by BMW drivers more than once. She turned her attention back to Tink who was focussed on the tarmac.

"I think we came to that one on our own," Tink yelped, pulling the wheel back into the left lane as a Greggs lorry rounded the corner. "But we're there now, Annie, let's not beat ourselves up. We're detectives, that's what we do. We whittle down the evidence until we get to the right conclusion."

"And Raven is our conclusion?" Annie cried.

"It's looking that way." Tink hit the horn again, this time to scare away a pheasant who was pecking at the side of the road, contemplating in the way that only pheasants do about running in front of the car. It flapped and disappeared off into the verge.

"But I was so tunnel visioned that I didn't see what Raven was doing," Annie shouted over the car skidding around a corner.

And Annie still wasn't sure of what they knew and why they knew it. Was someone playing with them? Was Raven leading them in circles, taunting them with riddles and lies? She pinched the bridge of her nose with her free hand, trying to squash away the headache that was looming. Glancing at her watch to see it was coming up to ten am, nearly twelve hours since she last saw Swift.

Annie glanced over again at Tink as she navigated the narrow country roads back to the pier. The sun hit her face through the windshield and she looked broken. Her hands white on the wheel, her face sagging with exhaustion. Tink's grief was sitting on her shoulders, weighing her down to a broken facade. Tink and Page had known Swift a lot longer than Annie had; they were feeling his absence as hard, if not harder, than she was. There was a great, aching void where Swift used to sit and Annie wasn't sure she could concentrate when that void was growing exponentially with each minute Swift stayed missing.

The sea came into view over the horizon, the sun illuminating the white capped waves and the darker depths.

"I see the sea," Annie whispered, remembering back to the first case she worked on in MCU and the way both she and Swift had raced to say it, despite not knowing each other. Now, the view of the sea made Annie feel sea sick. Tossed around in imaginary waves picturing Swift's body as he sank to the bottom. Annie shook her head. She placed a hand on Tink's arm as the DS pulled the car into the carpark. "We're going to get back to Raven and we're going to pummel her for information until she tells us where he is."

"Quite literally pummel her, if she's not careful," Tink replied, killing the engine, and sucking in air like she'd been holding her breath the whole way. "Grab your car and I'll meet you back at the station. I'm going to need restraining.

TINK WASN'T WRONG. ANNIE WASN'T SURE HOW either of them were going to get through the interview without leaping over the table and holding Raven to ransom for information about the DI.

Raven, on the other hand, looked as though she'd spent ten years in their cells and not ten hours. Her red hair was lank and stuck to her pasty skin with grease. The makeup she'd been wearing when she was brought in had long since rubbed away and she looked younger without it. Annie sat still, watching Raven as she picked at her chapped lips with her teeth, the skin peeling off with a blossom of blood.

Annie had driven back from the theatre as fast as she'd dared, which was still a lot slower than Tink. All the while, Annie's brain was whirring with the whos and the whys. Madame Seraphina had said that 'secrets are what create the mystery and without the secrets there is no magic.' She had also said that Mirage had lost his ethics for a girl, perhaps a bad choice of phrase and maybe it had been Seraphina who'd misdirected them. But Annie had to take some responsibility for where her mind had wandered, people used *girl* when they meant *woman* all the time, a throwback to the misogyny of life, she supposed.

All the same, Mirage had lost his ethics for a woman. For Raven? That made no sense, they were part of the same magic circle and Madame Seraphina had specifically said they all shared their tricks amongst each other. Which meant that Mirage would not have been black balled from The Veiled Order for sharing his secrets with Raven. So Raven couldn't have been the woman he'd lost his ethics over, could she?

So who was?

Did Raven find out Mirage was seeing someone else? Was there the shock of not only the cheating but the spilling of their secrets to an outsider? Did Raven kill Mirage because she was jealous? That age old motive. The Raven sitting opposite Annie looked like she had seen the end of the world and was merely waiting for it to hit.

"You need to start talking and you need to do it fast," Annie said, once Tink had hit the recorder and checked again that Raven didn't want legal representation. "We know you and Mirage were in a relationship. We also know Mirage was spilling magic secrets to someone not in The Veiled Order and that's why he was kicked out."

Raven picked at her lip some more.

"How long had you and Mirage been an item?" Tink asked.

Raven shrugged.

"Okay, let's try something different." Tink shifted in her chair, elbows on the table. "I would have thought you'd have had enough time to think about your situation while you were sat in your cell. But it would seem not. Isabelle, do you know what happens to people who hurt police officers when they're sent away?"

Raven's eyes widened but she kept quiet.

"Let's just say your face won't be your best asset anymore."

Tink was going too far. Annie shook her head at the young DS almost imperceptibly, but enough to feel the force of her death stare.

"Did Mirage threaten to leave you?" Annie tried. "Did he tell you he'd met someone else?"

Still Raven was tight lipped. Annie could feel her own blood pumping around her head, her throat restricted with the anger that had almost reached boiling point.

"Were you so jealous of Mirage having a relationship with someone else that you couldn't stand it and you locked him in his vanishing cabinet and poisoned him? Is that why? You're a scorned lover. A woman who couldn't bear to be thrown aside like garbage."

Even as Annie was saying it, she wasn't sure she could picture Raven as a cold-blooded killer. The woman looked barely strong enough to lift her own head, let alone trick a man to get in a cabinet and then fill it with gas. But Annie had been tricked before and she was damned if she'd be tricked again. Annie pressed on.

"You killed a man who you loved because you thought if you couldn't have him, no one else was going to? Is that how it happened?"

"I didn't kill Keith," Raven cracked. "You've got this all wrong. I loved Keith."

"Loved him enough to take his life?" Tink added. "What's the saying? If you love someone let them go. If you love someone show them that by plucking out their eyes and throwing them to the wolves."

"No."

Annie wasn't sure how, but Raven looked even paler than she had at the start of the interview. Her face was drawn, her eyes full of fear, as though she'd just realised the extent of the trouble she was in.

"Did you blind him so he could no longer see the other woman?" Annie asked, sickened.

"Don't. Stop. Please." Raven rocked in her chair. "His eyes? What do you mean blinded? Mirage was… he always saw things others didn't. He wasn't blind. He was the opposite."

Either she hadn't known about the damage to Mirage's eyes or she was putting on a good show. And why make a point about Mirage seeing everything? Was it an excuse for her behaviour?

"We know what happened to Mirage," Tink said, ignoring Raven's pleas. "So why don't you tell us what you've done with Swift? DI Swift. I swear, if you don't, I'm going to climb out of this chair and force it out of you. Swift is a *good* man."

Raven's body moved back and forth, the plastic seat creaking under her feather weight with the force of the movement. She hummed under her breath, Annie guessed it was to try and block out the anger that she and Tink were emitting, and not for the first time wondered if they were the best people to be in the room. They were too close to the case. They had too much invested in finding Swift. Maybe Raven could sense this and that was making her scared. She wasn't going to talk if they kept threatening her.

Maybe Raven needed a change of tack.

Annie drew in a ragged breath, trying to gain control

over her limbic system. She was in danger of losing it and that wouldn't do Mirage or Swift any favours. Almost as though Raven could feel the change of energy in the room, her eyes cast towards Annie's with a darkness in them that made Annie's blood run cold.

"We looked over your riddle again," Annie said, before Tink could throw anymore threats in Raven's direction. "But we think you're tripping us up and deliberately throwing us off course. This riddle is nothing but a few words put together that rhyme. Clever, but what is their purpose? You want to be a poet now magic is no longer open to you?"

Raven's lips narrowed and she shook her head in short sharp bursts. "Magic is my life."

"So you're not bluffing?" Annie's brain whirred with a thought that just wouldn't quite connect. "Why not just talk to us then? Tell us exactly what you need to, rather than writing it out in a riddle that makes absolutely no sense. I swear, if we don't get to Swift in time to save him because of your stupid riddle then…"

"I can't." Raven screamed, cutting Annie's sentence before she could divulge exactly what she'd do to the woman.

The room echoed with the cries. Annie's ear rang. Raven drew a ragged breath and slammed her palms down on the table.

"You can," Annie hissed, leaning in towards her. "And you will."

"I can't." Raven was full on sobbing. "You don't get it. I can't just tell you what I know."

And then it hit Annie like a steam train. She fell back in her chair.

"You can't tell us because to do so would mean telling us The Veiled Order secrets?" she said, not quite believing it. "You're willing to sacrifice a good man to stay in their circle?"

"They're not just my circle, they're my family." Raven dropped her head into her hands and broke down.

NINETEEN

ANNIE REALISED THE GRAVITY OF WHAT RAVEN HAD just said.

Of course she did.

She knew there was nothing quite like the sanctity of a family bond, despite her own failings in that area.

Raven looked like a woman who'd trekked the deserts or climbed Everest. Exhausted, but with a sense of relief about her. How long had she been keeping her relationship with Mirage secret? Let alone the ties she was bound by in The Veiled Order. The weight of them had been tethering Raven to a concrete block and now she was chiselling away at it to be free.

Annie felt broken, and from the looks of her, so did Tink.

"We need your help, Raven," Annie said, her own exhaustion hitting like a sledgehammer. Her eyes were so dry that every time she blinked it hurt. "I understand that you can't talk straight, but if there's anything you can tell us, please you have to."

Chances were that Raven didn't kill Mirage. Annie's instincts had proven right again, but her fear for Swift had overridden them.

"I grew up in a commune in Norfolk," Raven said, knocking Annie for six. If Madame Seraphina was her family, then the commune was most likely the same one she'd been leading. "My parents abandoned me when I was a toddler, so Sera took me under her wing. Everyone looked up to her, she was the pinnacle of power at home. Even though there were members who were much older than Sera, she has this way about her that people just can't help but listen to.

I loved growing up where I did. It was a huge family, a farm. We had cows and sheep and pigs, and I had brothers and sisters who weren't really related but we'd run around causing havoc all day. We were living on borrowed time, but we didn't know it back then."

Annie knew what was coming. Some of it, anyway. She braced herself against the backlash.

"Something happened," Raven went on. "When I was eleven. The police turned up. They were questioning all the adults, and they turned the place upside down. I had no idea what was going on, I guess as a child I was naive about how we could run this fantastic homestead with no apparent income. Now I realise that the police were probably raiding the farm for the giant greenhouses full of cannabis plants."

Annie balked, that wasn't what she'd been expecting. Cannabis hadn't been on her radar.

"What happened?" she asked.

"After it died down Sera left. I get why she left, but at the time it felt like I was being abandoned again. I *was* being abandoned again. I wanted to go with her, but she said I'd be better off staying with the commune. I was angry for so long that I forgot how to be happy. I took myself off and found this old magic set that had been left by Social Services when they came to visit. I think they left dvds and PlayStation games too, but we had no electricity in the houses most of the time, it was all being used to keep the plants warm and dry!

Anyway, I played and played with this set, hidden away behind the hay bales in the cow sheds, until I had mastered the tricks. They were pretty crude, mind you, but I loved them. I loved the way I could make things disappear or morph, though I wished I could do it to myself."

Annie shifted in her seat, her skills as a psychotherapist wearing thin when all she wanted to do was shake the information from Raven so she could sort it through herself. Pick out the bits that were important to finding Swift and nothing else.

"How did you and Sera rekindle your friendship?" Annie asked, not wanting to push, but she really didn't need to hear about Raven's teen years if they weren't relevant.

Raven shifted wearily on her chair.

"When I turned eighteen, I left the commune and rented a place in Wexwade. It was in the middle of nowhere and cheap. I got a job in the fish and chip shop to pay my way. I met Keith there, he was a Monday night regular; cod and chips with a side of mushy peas. Monday was his night off at the theatre and we got talking over magic and tricks. It was weird to meet someone else into what I was into. Especially in a place like Wexwade. He took me under his wing at first. He was married at the time so it was nothing like that, but Keith was a nurturer."

Annie felt the cogs turning in her head.

"Was he already a member of the Veiled Order then?"

Raven nodded. "Yeah, and when he got the all clear that I could join them I was so shocked to see that they were headed by Madame Seraphina, Sera."

"That's a pretty huge coincidence," Tink piped up, her arms crossed over her chest. "Given that magic isn't the most popular past time."

Raven scoffed.

"That's what I thought too," she said, her lips twisting. "In fact, that's what I said to both Keith and Sera. Turns out it wasn't so much a coincidence as Sera keeping an eye on me from afar. Apparently, she was in regular contact with the commune to find out how I was and what I was up to. When she found out I was practising magic she started to learn too. I mean, that's all very well, but why didn't she just contact me and ask how I was? It's a very convoluted way to stay in touch with a child who you promised to look after."

"So Sera set up The Veiled Order just so she could be close to you as an adult again?" Tink asked, sounding as incredulous as Annie felt.

"Yep," Raven replied, nodding. "And as weird as it sounds, this whole bloody thing, I joined and I felt like I was back with my family. And Sera has always been a leader, I think she was happy to take charge over a group of people again. I was part of something, an important part too. I have a knack for the good tricks and I loved it when people listened to me and took on board what I was showing them. I can't lose all that again, it would kill me."

"Which is why you can't tell us what you know?" Annie asked, though the question was rhetorical.

Raven nodded, looking at the table.

"When Keith was kicked out, I felt so sorry for him that I carried on going to see him. I know how it felt to be ostracised by the people you love. He was doing okay, he had Benjy and he'd recently taken on Candy as an assistant. We had to see each other on the down low though, so the Order didn't find out. Keith was so understanding about that. He told Benjy and Candy that I was trying to steal his tricks and that Benjy should keep away from me. That was sad, Benjy is a sweetheart, but we all have to make sacrifices. Candy was in a world of her own, learning the magic tricks, so she didn't take much notice of me, I don't think. But I kept out of her way all the same."

The cogs in Annie's brain clicked into place and she could see the train of thought that had been skitting about on the outskirts of her mind.

"It was Candy?" she said, abruptly. "Sorry, I didn't mean to interrupt you."

"And I don't mean to interrupt you both, but please excuse me for a moment, Evans is calling," Tink said, standing and taking the call, leaving the room. Annie updated the recording and carried on where she'd stopped.

"Keith had been training Candy, he was bound to have been telling her the secrets, how else could he help her to learn the tricks?" Annie thought back to how Swift had nurtured all of the staff in his team, how he'd trained Tink after spotting her in the academy. How he'd helped Annie regain her confidence after a false start in the police the first time around. Mirage and Swift were similar characters, and neither of them deserved what they had received.

Raven nodded.

"But surely if Mirage had told Madame Seraphina that he was training a new recruit she would have been more lenient about what he'd done?" Annie blurted.

"Keith was a stickler for the rules, always had been. He told Sera that he had accidentally given away some secrets but she didn't give him time to expand on that before she threw him out. Keith would never intentionally hurt the Order."

"Which is why you're so scared of talking?" Annie asked.

"Look how they treated him," Raven replied, wide eyed. "They ruined him. They warned everyone else against him, tried to bankrupt his shows by leaving hundreds of one-star reviews. They even used to hang out at the theatre to scare him. It was awful."

"Did Sera action all of that against Mirage?" Annie asked, seeing another side to the woman.

Raven nodded again.

"Sera has a streak to her, she's very much a reactive person. I can't have her doing the same to me."

Annie dropped her gaze to her fingers, surprised to see them white tipped where she was gripping her hands together so tightly.

"Is there anything you can tell us? What do you think happened to Mirage?" she asked.

"Keith had this trick that used a canister to create a loud explosion, he loved making the crowds jump. Maybe the whole poisoning was an accident." She shrugged.

"So why the riddle?"

"The riddle wasn't about Keith, it's about your friend."

"DI Swift?"

"Yes. I don't know what happened to Keith, but I did see something happen to DI Swift." Raven's eyes distorted with tears.

Annie's blood ran cold, she felt a violent shiver

wrack her body and she flinched as Tink sat back down next to her.

"Mirage scratched at his own eyes," Tink leant in to Annie and whispered. "Evans said they found evidence under his fingernails and there was no other DNA present. Carbon Monoxide toxicity can do that to a person."

"What?" Annie hissed back. "So we're thinking it was an accident now? That's what Raven just said too."

Tink shrugged, her mouth twisted.

"Raven was just telling me that the riddle had nothing to do with Mirage and was all about Swift," Annie brought Tink up to speed on the conversation she'd missed. With each word, the line between Tink's brow deepened.

"What did you see?" Annie asked, not wanting to lose the momentum the conversation had taken.

"I was in the theatre all day," Raven went on. "Hiding mostly from Benjy who was always keen to be around for show prep. After Keith... after it all happened, I hid out backstage and I heard you and the detective talking. I knew you'd found my card, which was in the vanishing cabinet because Keith liked something of mine around to keep him company. We had fun in that cabinet. Now it makes me feel sick. But when I saw you with the card I also knew you would look immediately at The Veiled Order and me in particular."

"So why didn't you show yourself, how did you hide so well?" said Annie.

"There was someone else there," Raven ignored the question. "I didn't see who, I just saw them with your DI. He was... I'm not sure if he was okay. Read the riddle. Read the second paragraph. Please don't make me say it out loud."

Annie's phone made her jump. She pulled it out of her pocket, almost glad of the distraction when Raven was making her want to punch someone.

> Meet me at the theatre. I need to show you something that might help you find your friend.

"It's Candy. Tink, is Page back yet?" Annie said, turning to her colleague.

"Not yet, his gran was confused with him being out all night." Tink drummed her fingers on the table, eyes not leaving Raven.

"Right, I need to go. I've got the riddle on my phone, call me if you get anywhere."

Annie heard Tink call after her but she couldn't wait, not after what Raven had just said. She grabbed her coat and ran out to the carpark.

TWENTY

ANNIE PULLED UP IN THE CARPARK TO TEN MISSED calls and a raft of messages from Tink. At first glance she thought something had happened, her mind immediately going to Swift. They'd found him. They had news. Bad news. Then she realised Tink was probably just a bit cranky at the way Annie had ghosted the interview at the drop of a hat. But they'd gotten all they were going to get from Raven, Annie understood that innate need to stay part of a family and do whatever it took to stay on their good side. Raven had lost her family twice now; she wasn't going to do it again.

Annie climbed out of her Golf and marched across the carpark to the pier. Underneath the wooden struts the sea had calmed. Instead of rising up against the legs like a kraken, the waves lapped gently, rhythmically. Annie's feet clip clopped in time to the waves all the way to the end of the pier and the door to the theatre. There was no police presence anymore. The divers were gone. The door was unguarded, wrapped instead in tape that floated in the gentle breeze. Tape that wasn't going to keep anyone out, including Annie.

"Candy?" Annie pushed the door open and called out into the foyer.

She dug her phone out, scrolling to the message that Candy had sent her. The young girl had just said she was at the theatre, so Annie shut the door behind her and stepped into the building. It felt like it had been empty for years, not just a few hours. A dampness settled in the walls and the floor, an icy chill crept up and wrapped itself around Annie's neck.

"Hello." She called again. "Is there anyone here?"

Annie tapped out a quick message to Candy, letting her know she had made it back to the theatre. Having no patience to sit and wait for a reply, Annie walked through the foyer and pushed open the double doors to the auditorium.

The vanishing cabinet stood sentry on the stage, a beast in size and stature. Really, now she'd seen the inside, Annie should have guessed at the secret door in the rear. It was all tricks of the eye and sleight of hand. Leading the audience to look at something, all the while covering your tracks while they were distracted. Had Mirage been trying to do just that with the Carbon Monoxide trick? Had he been planning a raft of mini explosions to distract his audience last night, and instead suffocated himself in a tiny box?

Annie felt the inkling of an idea blossom again in

her head. She thought back to last night, when Swift had seemingly vanished into thin air. She'd heard the doors to the vanishing cabinet open and close and had gone to investigate. Had that been a ruse to get her away from a real hiding place? Or did the Vanishing Cabinet hold a magic that Annie couldn't explain?

Annie took out her phone again, she was going to re-read the riddle, in particular the second paragraph like Raven had told her to, but the screen was lit up with Tink's face.

"Tink," Annie swiped to answer. "I'm sorry for leaving, don't be mad. Candy messaged to say she had something so show me."

"You're back at the theatre?" Tink was walking, Annie could hear her footsteps.

"Yeah, just got here," Annie went on. "Did you get anything else out of Raven?"

"No, she clammed up again," Tink said. "But that's not why I'm calling. Nor am I calling to moan at you. I get why you're there. Everyone does. Robins has sent a uniformed officer to Swift's house to see if there's anyone there that they need to inform. That's normally something we do immediately, but none of us did. And do you know why, Annie?"

"Um, no," Annie replied, poking the shoe of her toe into the skirting of the vanishing cabinet.

"Because we all know that everyone Swift cares about is at the station or the theatre searching for answers to where he has gone."

Annie thought about Swift and the way his island

of people was small. He really did care about his team, he cared about the way they worked together, yes, but he also cared about them as human beings. The only other person in his life, other than his team, was his mum, and Annie still didn't know a lot about the woman who brought him up. Tears welled in her eyes.

"Oh Tink," Annie said, sniffing. "Where is he? Why can't we find any trace of him except his stupid phone?"

"That reminds me," Tink said. Annie could hear her tapping away at her keyboard. "I called to talk to you about his phone. We need to get into it, I don't suppose Swift gave you his password, did he?"

Annie huffed out a laugh. "In what world can you see Swift handing out a password to anyone? Let alone me. Imagine what he's got on there."

"Just thought I'd try. Tech guys figured it was thrown or dropped inside the cabinet and are working on getting into it."

"Out of interest," Annie said, pulling the doors to the cabinet open and peering inside. It was dark, but enough daylight crept in for Annie to see the painted wall at the back and the high step up into it. "Why do the tech guys think it was dropped here?"

Tink stopped typing. "The giant crack down the screen. They said it must have been thrown with force or landed at a funny angle on something hard."

"Yeah it was," Annie's heart raced. "It was thrown at Sunday because the stupid cat was trying to pee in

Swift's bed. Only, of course Swift deliberately missed because he's not an utter knob, so his phone hit his nightstand instead. His nightstand is all metal and concrete, because in that sense he is a bit of a knob."

"You're saying his screen was already cracked?" Tink asked, her voice an octave higher than before.

"Yes."

"Shite."

"But it could still have been dropped?" Annie asked, stepping into the cabinet. Her words echoed in the space. "I mean, he could have been in here and dropped it and it just wasn't damaged because it slipped from his pocket."

"Swift's pockets are deep and normally full of crap." Tink was typing again, Annie pictured her rapidly hitting the keys. "If he dropped his phone then he would have dropped the wrappers that go with it."

"Nothing quite like an empty packet of Mentos to guide the way." Annie was almost talking to herself as she stepped deep into the cabinet, the door still wide open. "You don't think he was trying to tell us something, do you?"

Tink whistled through her teeth. "I wouldn't put it past Swift to leave a clue if he could. Why don't you go and have another look in the cabinet."

"Way ahead of you, Tink," Annie said, dropping to her haunches. "I'm in the cabinet as we speak."

It was dusty right at the back, Annie's knees brushing away two lines as she shuffled across the floor.

"I'm heading to the tech department to get back Swift's phone," Tink said from where Annie had left her own phone, propping open the hinges on the cabinet.

"Copy that," she called back. "Let me know when you've got it. I can't really see anything in here, it's a bit grubby."

"Check that," Tink shouted, obviously running. "Check the dirt on the walls and the floor."

Annie looked down at where her knees had rubbed tracks in the dust and suddenly felt alive. Of course. She swung her gaze back and forth over the floor and the walls, hoping beyond hope that the tracks from her knees hadn't worn away something vital. And that's when she saw it.

"Tink, it's here, I think I've got something," Annie yelled, spinning around and facing the back corner.

Annie bent backwards and grabbed her phone, hitting the torch and sending the gloomy corner into a spotlight of white. There, written in the dust was a number 0408.

"Zero, four, zero, eight," Annie said. "That's it. That must be his code. Swift left his phone for us to find, and he must have left his code here because there's something on that phone that we need."

"I'm nearly there," Tink said, huffing and out of breath. "We're coming for you Swift. We're coming."

Tink went quiet and Annie shuffled again to get comfortable. Rearranging her legs under her, Annie span around and came face to face with the inside of the doors.

"What?" She pushed against them. They wouldn't budge. They must have clicked shut when she moved her phone. Annie's heart pounded in her throat as she grappled for the handle. "Er, Tink, I think I'm trapped."

"That's great," Tink said, sounding like she hadn't really heard what Annie had said. "Annie, that's it, I'm into his phone, Annie. It's opened straight to his notes app. Hold on, let me just…"

There was silence, followed by the annoying beeps that happened every time Swift pressed a key because he hadn't yet turned off that function, followed by the unmistakeable sound of Swift himself. Annie inhaled sharply and listened, with an ache deep in her bones, to the whispered recording.

"O'Malley, listen, I haven't got long." Swift sounded like a teen on a night out pretending to be sober. "I've been locked in the cabinet and I feel awful. I'm not sure if it's Carbon Monoxide or some other drug. I'm leaving my phone. I hope you find it… well actually if you're listening to this then you've found it. And found the code. Fourth August, Annie, the day that changed my whole life." Swift was wracked with a rattling cough, clawing for breath he tried to carry on. "You need to get out of the theatre, it's not safe, there're secrets everywhere. You need to get to the little boy, Annie," Swift coughed again, his voice sounding weaker. "Get to

Benjy. Stop him…" Annie heard the thud of Swift falling and her hand flew over her mouth to stem the sob. "Stop… him… going… to… his… mum's. It's her."

The recording went quiet. Neither Tink nor Annie spoke. Annie felt like she'd been run over by a truck and it had reversed for good measure. Swift had spent his last breath of that call making sure the others around him knew who to look for.

"Why didn't he call for help?" Tink cried over the phone, startling Annie. "Annie, why didn't he just call you and get you to let him out?"

"He couldn't," Annie said, sniffing. "His phone had no reception here. So he did the only thing he could think of to help us."

She kicked at the doors in anger

"We need to find Zoe," she went on, trying to stay focussed. If Swift could sacrifice everything to leave them a giant arrow pointing to their perp, Annie wasn't going to waste that. "Get a team on it, Tink. Go and pick her up and bring her in. I need to call Candy and get her to come and rescue me from this bloody great puzzle box… oh god, Tink, I think I know what Raven meant. Read me the second paragraph of her riddle."

Tink cleared her throat and Annie heard papers rustling.

"Through trapdoors and secret panels, the magician cast their spell, but when the curtains part once more, the mystery deepens, oh so well. With robes of velvet, wands in hand, they vanish into air, leaving behind a mystery, a puzzle oh so rare."

"That's it," Annie said, pulling herself up to standing. "What's the rarest puzzle, the oldest puzzle? A puzzle box. I think that's what Raven meant when she said concentrate on the second paragraph and we'd know what happened to Swift."

"What?"

"Swift was in this cabinet, yes?" Annie went on. "We just heard that and I *knew* I saw someone in here when I was looking for him. I saw them shut the door but when I looked it was empty. What if it wasn't empty? What if the puzzle box *is* the cabinet? Through trapdoors and secret panels. There's more than one hiding place. Tink, I need to hang up. You call Candy and tell her I'm trapped in here. Get her to come and let me out. She might know about the other secret panels too."

"On it," Tink said. "Annie, be careful."

TWENTY-ONE

THE VANISHING CABINET WASN'T IN ANY HURRY TO give up its secrets. It knew nothing of the pain that Annie was going through just to hold it together. It was a wooden structure with four sides and a roof and Annie needed to remind herself of this before she went at it with an axe. Not that she had an axe. Or any way out of the cabinet to get an axe. But right now, that was the least of her worries.

Swift had sounded so out of it that if it was Carbon Monoxide poisoning then the likelihood of him being okay this many hours later was zero. But that thought made Annie gag so she swallowed it down and went back to searching the cabinet for clues.

Outside, Annie had recognised that the cabinet was like a reverse Tardis, smaller inside than out. That's what had helped them find the secret door at the back. But now she was stumped. The ceiling height was the same outside and in, a pitched roof which was plain to see when she shone her torch on it. The floor had a slight step up from outside, but nothing deep enough to hide a human. Especially a Swift sized human. She felt methodically around the walls, looking for lumps and bumps that might push or twist to reveal more secrets.

What was it the riddle said? Trapdoors and panels, vanish into air, mystery deepens. The clue was there; Annie knew it was staring her in the face and she couldn't grasp it because all she could think about was the way Mirage had scratched his own eyes out at the pain caused by the Carbon Monoxide. Had Swift's eyes burned so badly that he'd wanted to gouge them from his face too? His blue eyes that saw everything and gave away nothing. Hidden depths, just like the bloody cabinet.

"God dammit, Annie, focus," she shouted, thumping the wall and feeling something shift inside her brain like a key turning in a lock. The tumblers turned and clicked into place.

Trapdoors.

Deepens

Vanish.

Annie had it, she knew what it was. The secret wasn't another hidden space *inside* the cabinet, it was a trapdoor out of it. Zoe must have seen Annie coming up from under the stage and used another exit before she found Swift. Hope blossomed in her chest as she realised that without the confines of the cabinet walls, the Carbon Monoxide suffocating Swift might have dispersed quickly enough for him to still be okay.

She dropped to her hands and knees and felt across the floor. It had to be something quick to find and even quicker to activate if Mirage used it for his show. The floor felt rough under her fingers, splinters from the wood pushed their way painfully between her nails and their beds but the need for answers had taken hold of her and she barely felt it.

The tips of her fingers jolted against an edge, bruising the skin. Annie felt along the sides of the raised section, just high enough to stick up, low enough to not be obvious. She found all the sides, oblong, slightly larger than her foot. Pressing it down, Annie heard a click.

"Got you," she said, waiting. But nothing happened. There was no grand opening, no swinging of a trapdoor showing Annie the way to freedom. "What? Come on. Come on."

Annie pressed it again. Maybe she hadn't pressed hard enough the first time. Something in the depths of the cabinet clicked again but the noise was the only sign anything was happening. She stood up, balancing on one foot and pressing her whole weight through the button. The same. Annie dropped her other foot down at the same time she realised what she needed to do. Having one button to open a trap door is dangerous. What if Mirage had accidentally stood on it while he was shifting around in the dark?

Feeling around with her other foot, Annie found the second button, she stood on them both together and waited.

The cabinet clicked. A gap of light filtered up through the floor where a square section had dropped open by a few inches. Annie crouched to her knees and unclipped the hatch, letting it swing open on its hinges, a rope ladder dropping into the room below.

The storage room.

Annie pocketed her phone and dropped her legs over the edge, finding the rungs of the ladder and carefully lifting herself onto it. Climbing down, Annie could feel the sharp drop in temperature. She could hear the waves as they hit against the legs of the pier. Her phone rang; thinking it might be Candy, Annie looped her arm through the ladder and pulled it from her pocket, seeing the young girl's name on the screen.

"It's okay, Candy, I'm out," she said, feeling a bit seasick with the movement of the ladder.

"It took you long enough to work it out," the reply came.

"Candy?" Annie looked at her screen again. It definitely said Candy, but Annie didn't recognise the voice as hers.

A slow clap echoed across the room, bouncing off the low ceiling and thundering loudly through Annie's phone. She flinched, holding it away from her ear with the pain of the clap, her foot slipped on the rung, she clung to the rope, letting go of her phone which crashed to the floor with a sickening crack. The clapping continued.

"Candy?" Annie shouted out, regaining her composure and finding her feet. She slid to the bottom of the ladder and looked up. The trapdoor had snapped shut behind her. "Candy, are you down here?"

The clapping was unsettling her. Its rhythm too slow, too deliberate. She wondered if it was the sound of the waves coming from the fire exit door. It was wide open, a mouth to the sea, gaping and toothless. Boxes lined the room, not as many as there had been before, but enough to hide the dark corners and conceal a person who didn't want to be seen.

Annie looked around, hugging her arms to her body to stop the shivering. She picked up her phone, seeing through the cracked screen that she had five missed calls from Tink and a message. Trying to swipe to open it, nothing happened, the screen was too badly damaged. Annie read what she could of the message, backing away from the open door to the sea.

Get out Annie. Paperwork back from uniform shows Zoe was sectioned for trying to hurt Mirage. We can't get hold of Candy and Zoe's not at home. You're in dang

Annie didn't need to read the rest to know what Tink was going to say. She span on her toes and started to run towards the door to the stage and the freedom of the theatre.

"Leaving without saying goodbye?" The voice was as cold as the air.

Annie stopped in her tracks. Her hackles rose, tickling her neck and wriggling through her hair.

"Zoe," she said, turning slowly.

"Mrs Stuckley, to you." Zoe rose from the shadows, poised. She looked the same as she had done when Annie had talked to her at home. The same, except for the way her eyes bore into Annie with so much hatred she felt her stomach drop out from under her.

"Mrs Stuckley," Annie replied. "I'm going to open this door and head out into the theatre to wait for my colleagues to arrive. They're on their way and they know where I am. I suggest you come with me too."

Zoe laughed. Annie couldn't feel the cold anymore, her whole body was numb.

"Your colleagues are still at the station," Zoe said, coolly. "One of them called me, not that long ago. Called Candy too, but she's a bit preoccupied."

Zoe held up her hands, a phone in each one.

"It was you who messaged me, from Candy's phone?" Annie asked. "You lured me out here. Why?"

Zoe stepped back towards the fire escape, eyes not leaving Annie.

"I could see how much *he* meant to you, thought you might like to say goodbye," she said, shrugging. "I understand the pain of having a loved one taken without being able to say goodbye."

"Mirage?"

"Do me a favour," Zoe scoffed. "That man couldn't lose me even if he tried. I've been watching him, you know. Waiting for a good moment to play him at his own game. He sent me away, did you know that?"

Annie shook her head, her mind racing to put together all the pieces. She remembered Seraphina saying Zoe had left the town for a while after she split with Mirage. From what Tink had found, Zoe hadn't left of her own accord.

"Sent you where, Zoe?" Annie was inching closer to Zoe, closer to the open door.

"Got me locked away. Said it was for my own good because I was a danger to myself and…" Zoe's voice hitched in her throat. "Me! I was a danger? I was the sanest one in this god-awful family."

"That must have been hard for you," Annie said, taking another small step.

Zoe screeched like a banshee. "HARD. You wouldn't know the meaning of hard. He took everything from me. My home. My life. My son. Well I wasn't going to sit back and let Mirage have everything I worked hard for. He's my son too."

Benjy.

This whole thing was about Benjy. There was no secret cult, no magic gone wrong, no Veiled Order members teaching Mirage a lesson. This was about family and the hurt that comes with loving someone and losing them.

"You killed him to have access to your son?"

"I wasn't going to let him take my son away again. Not after last time." Zoe's eyes narrowed. "I can see you moving, you know. I may have been locked away but I'm not stupid."

"I don't for a minute think you're anything other than razor sharp, Zoe." Annie shook her head. "No one else could have made it this far without the police realising what they'd done. No one else could have stolen one of our own out from under our noses."

Zoe laughed again, the smile not reaching her eyes.

"You should have seen yourself, running around like headless chickens the lot of you. *Swift, oh Swift, where are you?* Annie's fists clenched, she could feel her nails digging into her palms.

"And if you'd only searched thoroughly more than once, you might have found him," Zoe went on. "He needed to be found, you know? When you decided to look in the vanishing cabinet I had to drop him quickly. His face got a little bashed up, but it was his arm I was mostly worried about. Still, he doesn't need to worry about that now, does he?"

"Where is he?" Annie stepped up, there was a row of boxes between the two women and not much else. "What did you do with him?"

It was the slight twitch of Zoe's head towards the sea that gave her away. Annie felt bile rise in her throat, acidic and burning. She glanced at the woman and glanced at the door, lunging towards it before she could change her mind.

The metal staircase creaked with the weight and the sudden movement. Annie gripped the rail so hard her fingers went completely white. Below her the sea had risen, waves thrashing up the stairs towards her like they were being riled by her anger.

"WHERE IS HE?" she screamed, and then she felt her legs buckle underneath her. "Swift?"

His body lay prone, wedged between the stairs and the length of steel girder holding them to the pier. The waves lapped over his face and his body, threatening to pull him under. His right arm was bent awkwardly underneath him, his leg bloody through his jeans. There was a huge gash across his forehead, caked in blood, and his eyes were black and bruised. But Swift wouldn't have been able to open his eyes even if they weren't swollen shut, Annie could tell that by the way his body was lifted limply with each wave.

"He wasn't supposed to get stuck," Zoe shrugged from inside the theatre. "But he'll be gone soon enough."

"You said you called me here to say goodbye." Annie screamed over the waves. "Why call me at all if you were going to throw him to the sea?"

"Oh, I wasn't planning on pushing him over the edge, only when your colleagues called me I thought I'd better get on with it. I can overpower one of you, but not a whole team. Hit his head hard on the way down, no coming back from that. And that's on you, that is. It's your fault he's down there, though I wasn't planning on him getting stuck." Zoe laughed.

Annie looked back down at Swift as the sea tried once again to take him. She needed to get to him, she needed to retrieve his body. There was no way Annie could let Swift be swept away to oblivion. Taking it as fast as she dared, Annie stepped across the platform and placed a foot on the stair below.

"Are you sure you want to do that?" Zoe asked.

Annie ignored her.

"Look," Zoe said, louder this time.

Annie turned her head and saw that Zoe was pointing to the top of the metal fire exit. Looking up, Annie felt her head swim. It was Candy; arms and legs tied, gagged, petrified, and Annie could see why. One wrong move and Candy would fall. And there was no way she would survive the drop.

TWENTY-TWO

THE WORLD TILTED ON ITS AXIS AND ANNIE FELL WITH it, dropping to the icy metal platform. Her knees popped painfully as the non-slip grips ripped at her jeans and skin. Warmth flooded them but Annie couldn't waste time patching up bloody knees when she had a decision to make.

Life or death. Candy or Swift.

Anger filled Annie like lava in a volcano and she burst open, screaming at Zoe.

"Why Candy? All she's ever done is look after that little boy of yours." Annie felt the spray of the sea and saw Swift being lifted higher than before. She gripped the rail and watched as the sea set him carefully back down.

All the while she was standing arguing with Benjy's mum, Swift was being moved towards a watery grave. But he might already be dead, he was pale, motionless despite the cold water splashing his face. Candy was young, she had the rest of her life to play out. Swift wouldn't want Annie to prioritise his safety over that of a teenage girl.

"She's trying to be his mother," Zoe spat. "Candy will take Benjy away from me, just you see. She's no better than Mirage. They're both liars, they do it for a living. Magic is just an immoral way to fool people. Benjy wouldn't even sit on my lap when he finally came home. What boy doesn't want to sit in his mother's lap? It's *her* fault. She's poisoned him against me."

Up above their heads, Candy wrestled with her restraints, her eyes bloodshot and wide. She jerked her body and slipped closer to the edge of the girder. Annie saw red.

"What about you? You were locked away for trying to kill Mirage and as soon as you're free you do it. You killed Mirage, and you've blamed everyone for what's happened except yourself," Annie shouted, stumbling to her feet and starting toward Zoe.

"Because it's *not my fault*," Zoe screamed, spittle flying from her lips.

She leapt out of the theatre doors and onto the platform, a blood-chilling wail emitting from her like an emergency beacon. Annie felt the stairs move again with the shift in weight and jolted to one side, reaching out and grabbing the rails to stop herself being flung over the edge. It was a small move, a simple one really, but it was enough to knock Annie out of Zoe's path as she ran at her, arms outstretched as if she was going to grab Annie's throat and squeeze it until it popped. In the blink of an eye, Zoe was gone. Toppling over the railings with the momentum of her hatred and plummeting into the dark waters below, hitting her head with a sickening thud on the way down.

Annie held her breath as the impact splashed causing a ripple of waves toward Swift, lifting him higher from the girder. The heavy weight of his legs pulling him away from safety. Above her Candy cried out through her gag.

"Candy, don't move," Annie called, making a split-second decision that she knew would change the rest of her life. "Stay perfectly still, I'm coming up."

Dragging herself to her feet, Annie pulled her body towards the stairs heading to the pier, her shoes clanging on the metal. Annie didn't want to look down, she couldn't live with herself watching Swift get taken out to sea. She focussed on the young girl who needed her and not the sobs that were forcing their way up her throat. Annie looked up again, seeing the pain in Candy's eyes, and started to run towards her.

"It's okay, Candy, it's okay. Swift wouldn't want you to die too." Annie ran to the top, her lungs burning, her legs like the steel girders themselves.

She reached the top, white stars speckling her vision. Annie knew she was running on empty after so long without sleep or proper food, her body wanted to fold in on itself with grief that hadn't completely registered yet. But Candy was only a few feet away, across the girder stretching over between the top of the stairs and the pier. A mirror image of what was below, only Candy was awake and talking and scared.

Annie ducked under the rails and knelt on the bar, her knees hot and painful like a heel blister perpetually rubbed by a hard shoe. She edged slowed across the girder, ignoring the raging sea below. Candy's arms were bound behind her back with duct tape, her ankles wrapped together. If she moved too far one way or another she would plummet to the sea, hitting the stairs on her way because she had no way of reaching out and stopping herself. Annie inched ever closer, feeling the wind whip around her hair. She was nearly there; Candy's hands were within touching distance.

"I'm going to free your hands now, Candy," she said, letting the girl know she was close. "Try not to move."

With freezing fingers, Annie tore at the tape around Candy's wrists. The young girl's hands were white with lack of blood. The tape was sticky and tightly wrapped and Annie couldn't get purchase, her fingers were too slippery with sea spray and sweat.

"I'm nearly there, Candy," Annie said, softly, mind whirring for a solution to present itself. "Try not to look down."

She had no phone, no keys to use, nothing sharp in her pockets to slice away the restraints. Annie clenched her jaw, the sea goading her from below.

He's mine.

He's mine.

"But Candy won't be," Annie called back, pushing her face into the back of Candy and ripping away the tape with her teeth.

The tape caught her lip, peeling it off painfully where Annie had been biting nervously at it. Tears pricked her eyes, coating her cheeks when she blinked them away to see the last of the tape snapping free. Annie gripped the loose end and pulled.

"Sorry," she called as a warning. "There's no time."

She ripped the tape away from Candy's arms, wincing with guilt as she took hair and skin with it. Candy wriggled her hands free, crying out as she pulled the scarf away from her mouth and started tugging at the tape binding her feet. Her position was still precarious, but at least she could now stop herself from falling.

"I'm so sorry," Candy called out. "It's my fault, I bought those firecrackers to scare away Zoe, I'd seen her watching the theatre. Zoe must have found them and used them to kill Keith. If I hadn't have bought them, Keith would still be alive."

"That's not true, Candy," Annie called back, holding Candy's shoulders as she untied her feet. "Keith didn't die because of the firecrackers, Zoe poisoned him. You were just looking out for Benjy. You did well, Candy. You're a good person."

"So is Swift," Candy called, grunting with the

effort of undoing the tape. "Your friend told me to get away. He's the only reason Zoe didn't push me into the sea too."

"What do you mean?" Annie cried. "I thought Swift died when she pushed him off the staircase."

Annie daren't look down. She didn't want to see the empty girder where Swift had been lying. She didn't want to think about his injured body sinking to the depths of the North Sea.

"He *was* alive, Annie," Candy called over her shoulder. "Very much alive. I'm only up here because Swift distracted Zoe for long enough for me to get away. I shouldn't have left him. I'm sorry. I'm so sorry. If I'd not hidden here, if only I'd gone up further then you wouldn't have had to save me instead of him."

Swift was alive?

Annie jolted as Candy's legs came free. Both women tilted to the side, reaching across to the supporting beam to stop themselves from falling. Annie faced the water, arms screaming at her to push back onto the girder. Beneath the stairs, she could just make out the shape of Swift's final hurrah as a wave lifted him completely. Barely able to think, Annie gripped at the support with her hands and swung down from the girder completely, hanging from her hands.

"Go home, Candy, wait for the police," Annie shouted. "Benjy is going to need you."

"Annie, what are you doing," Candy cried back,

scooting across the beam towards the stairs. "You'll never make it. There's concrete under the legs of the pier."

"I have to try." Annie sobbed.

Candy screamed as Annie let go. Annie couldn't have screamed if she'd wanted to. The drop was over in a split second, the icy water gripping her chest and freezing her head. She gasped, inhaling a lungful of the sea, and tried to pull herself back to the surface. But the water was strong and her wet clothes were heavy. She was sinking. Annie threw her eyes open, the pain like glass shards puncturing her retinas. She looked around, the water clearer than she'd expected.

Yet she was still sinking.

The concrete was deep enough for her to miss, though how she didn't hit a metal beam on the way down, Annie would never know. And then she saw it. A flash of white in the gloom. Swift's trainers.

Kicking with all her might, Annie focussed on the beacon in the distance and not the ache in her lungs. He was just past the leg of the pier and falling. She kicked and pulled at the water, trying to slosh it behind her, anything to move forwards. The pier loomed nearer and Annie grabbed at it. The metal bit into her fingers, blood pooled in the water. For a split second Annie had the vision of a shark biting away her bloody hand. But the prospect of drowning was a more obvious path to death and the shark vanished. Pretty stars blinkered Annie's eyes, sparkling white like Swift's trainers.

Swift. Focus Annie.

Keeping one hand on the sharp metal leg, Annie reached out as far as she could towards the sinking body of Swift. Something brushed her fingers and she gripped, in a flash and pincer-like. The stars were encroaching on the centre of Annie's vision, her heart pounded, her lungs felt like they were being compressed in a meat grinder.

Hold on. Just a few more seconds.

Annie tugged her catch towards her. The palm gripping the pier sank further into the metal, but she had him. She had the edge of his shirt and she wasn't letting go. Pulling with all her might, Annie inched her way upwards. The sun was teasing through the tips of the waves. Not far. Not far to go. But Annie wasn't sure she was going to make it. Any second now her lungs would automatically inflate and there was nothing she could do to prevent the respiratory system overriding her will to live.

Her vision faded to black, the surface so tantalising close yet so horribly far. Annie knew it was time. She'd tried. She'd saved Candy. She would now sink to the floor with Swift where they could lay together until their team found their bodies. She felt sad for Mim, sad for Rose her best friend and confidant, sad for Sunday the cat who'd be at home meowing for his food if not for her, sad that she never got to the bottom of the twisted tale between her parents, and sad for the missed chances between her and the man whose shirt she had gripped in her fingers.

The man whose eyes had just burst open.

Shocked into action. Annie and Swift gave one final push to the surface, clawing in air over the top of the waves. Annie gulped in as much as she could, the muscles in her chest contracting painfully around her ribs.

"Swift," she coughed, bobbing over the waves as they splashed her face. "You're okay?"

He wasn't okay, far from it. His face looked like it was made from putty and even without the drenching from the sea Annie knew it would be damp. A trail of spit dangled from his lips. He was barely afloat and one of his arms was hanging lower than it should be.

"Well, you're not dead, at least," Annie grimaced.

"Please don't make me laugh," Swift coughed and spluttered. "I think I've broken my ribs."

"You've broken a lot more than your ribs," Annie said, putting a gentle hand on the scar across his nose, leaving a trail of blood from her fingers.

"Not the face," Swift said, giggling like a madman who'd been brought back from the dead and was only just realising it. "Please, not the face."

He turned onto his back to float better and yelped with the pain of the movement. The water was rough, knocking against the legs of the pier and crashing in all directions. But they were at the surface and they were breathing. Annie swam up behind Joe and cradled his head, her legs kicking wildly under the surface to keep them both afloat. They floated calmly for a minute before his head jolted up, nearly cracking Annie in the chin.

"Candy," he yelled before doubling over and sinking back down with the pain.

"It's okay, she's okay," Annie said, stroking his hair. "She's going home where she'll be safe."

Over the sounds of the waves a voice shouted out, "I'm not going anywhere."

Annie freed up an arm and guided their bodies towards the shouts. It was Candy at the bottom of the fire escape, hand outstretched for Annie. In the distance the wail of the sirens was getting louder. Help was coming. Help was already here. Annie's breath shuddered in her chest as she finally let the tears break free. They were safe and Swift was alive.

TWENTY-THREE

ANNIE AWOKE FEELING LIKE SLEEPING BEAUTY AFTER a hundred years of slumber. Sunlight streamed in through her blinds and Sunday purred in her face from his own bed on her chest. She scritched his chin and booped his nose with her own until she realised where she was. It wasn't sunlight through blinds, it was strip lights glaring down on her face. It wasn't Sunday weighing her down, it was a Bair Hugger, a heated blanket designed to wrap hospital patients at the cusp of hypothermia in warmth.

She sat up, quickly sliding back down under the blue blanket as her head throbbed in a way that made her eyeballs pulsate. The eyeless face of Mirage flashed across her closed lids and, with it, the memory of the last god-knows-how-many days crashed down.

"Swift?" Annie's voice sounded like Barry White. She coughed and cleared away the hoarseness. "Swift?"

A hand rested on her arm, warm and comfortingly heavy.

"You're up before me," Annie croaked. "How'd you manage that?"

"It's not Swift," said the owner of the hand, shifting in the plastic seat with a creak.

Annie peeled open an eye, waiting for the samba band to start drumming again in her head.

"Page," she said, surprised. "So good to see you. How's your gran?"

"Trust you to be asking after the health of someone else when you're the one wrapped in a hospital bed wrapped up in what looks like a form of medieval torture," Page replied. "But thanks, she's okay. Her weekly carers are in and she's settled."

"What day is it?" Annie remembered heading to the magic show on the Friday night but she had little clue how many days had passed since. She was also putting off asking the question she most wanted to, because she was scared what the answer might be.

"Monday," Page said. "Start of a new work week. The office is a bit quiet though. Tink said I should come here because I was making too much noise with my silence, whatever that means."

Page laughed softly.

"Sounds like Tink," Annie laughed too. "Do you know when I can get out? I have a cat at home who's probably eating his way through my cupboard doors to get to his food."

"Later today," Page said. "Doctors just need to

check your core temperature and write up your prescription, apparently."

"How's Swift?" Annie couldn't wait any longer.

A shadow fell over the bay, person sized through the curtain. It opened and Mim slid in through the small gap.

"He's sleeping," Mim said, nodding hi to Page and kissing Annie on the forehead.

Page rose and offered Mim his chair, sliding through the gap in the curtain and back out into the busy A&E. Annie almost jumped out of bed to go with him, but she was attached at the arm to a drip and the Bair Hugger was too cosy.

"Mim," Annie said, coolly.

Mim dropped into the vacated seat and took Annie's hand, giving it a gentle squeeze.

"Annie, I'm so sorry." Mim was fidgety. "I was drunk when you called about Sera. I shouldn't have said what I did." She got up and paced the small space between Annie's bed and the curtain. "In all honesty, I can't really remember much of what I did say. But I'm sure it was all nonsense."

Annie didn't want to go over the debate about what Mim did with Swift, not again. Her sister was young and, from the small time she'd been back in Annie's life, seemingly pretty reckless.

"Sera told me she was working undercover with Dad," Annie said.

Mim stopped mid step, her face creasing.

"What?" She sat back down. "Sera wasn't police. She was the cult leader."

"Nope." Annie shook her head. "Dad was Sera's boss. I don't know what she was doing there, or how she managed to work her way up to the top of the food chain, but she did. Did Dad take you to see her when you left?"

"I was three years old, Annie," Mim replied. "I have no idea."

"But you knew about her?" Annie prompted.

"Yeah, only cos Dad used to talk about her all the time."

"I think Dad and Sera were having an affair," Annie said.

Mim laughed. "Wouldn't surprise me. He had a string of women around the country, a broken heart in every place we moved to."

"Then why didn't you go there when Dad took you away?"

"Like I said, Annie, I was three. We may very well have gone straight to Sera, but I can't remember."

"You didn't. Sera said when Dad left she never saw him again. That's weird, right? Especially if they were having an affair. Apparently, Mum thought that's where you'd gone, she sent the MisPer team to the commune."

"Look, Annie," Mim sighed. "I know you want Dad to be the villain in your life story, but he isn't in mine. You can paint him in any way you like, you're not going to change my mind."

"I don't *want* him to be the villain, he *is* the villain. He upped and left me and I haven't seen him since."

"Well maybe now's the time." Mim stood up, crossing her arms over her chest.

"What?"

"Maybe you need to go and talk to him and have it out with him so you can stop taking your anger out on me."

"How can I do that? I've no idea where he is."

"I do," Mim said, pulling open the curtain. Outside it, the A&E buzzed with activity. "He's working as security in a locked hospital ward down south. I'll take you when you're out of here."

Mim didn't wait for a reply. She pulled the curtain shut behind her and left Annie alone with her Bair Hugger and a whole lot of thoughts. It was too much, Annie felt like she couldn't breathe. She sat up, ignoring the jackhammer in her skull, and pulled off the weighted blanket. It slid to the floor with a thud, its wires and pipes taking the cotton blanket with it leaving Annie sitting in her underwear. She was wondering what had happened to her jeans and jumper when the curtain slid open again.

"I don't think it's a good idea you being here, right now," Annie said, anger pulsating in her face.

"Oh, sorry, I just wanted to check you were okay. I'll go."

Annie glanced around, her face lighting up as she saw Swift trying to manoeuvre himself back out the cubicle in his wheelchair. With one arm in a sling and one leg sticking straight out in front, he wasn't great at reversing. The wheels caught the curtain and threatened to topple the chair and bring down the rail on top of them both.

"Swift," Annie cried. "I thought you were Mim, please don't leave."

Swift gave the chair a great big push back towards the bed, pulling the curtain shut behind him. His bare toes poked out at the front of a plaster cast that covered his leg from hip to ankle. The hand propped up in the sling across his chest was blue and purple. His face was a similar colour, eyes swollen and bruised. Swift caught Annie looking.

"Dislocated shoulder and broken elbow," he said, motioning towards his arm. "Broken femur and ankle. Concussion. Hypothermia. And a sprinkling of tachycardia from the Carbon Monoxide. Zoe Stuckley trapped me in the cabinet and tried to poison me, I was sure I was going to die, but for some reason she opened the doors and climbed in. And thank god she did. I, stupidly, thought she was going to let me go but then I dropped into the basement and she left me unconscious behind a load of boxes until the coast was clear. It felt like a dream, Annie, like I could hear people walking above me but couldn't call out."

Annie felt her throat constrict. Her eyes stung with tears as a wave of emotion took hold of her. She leant over the bed and pulled up the hospital blanket from the floor, wrapping it round her shoulders and legs.

"Hypothermia." She shrugged, her voice breaking. "You win."

"Clearly," Swift smiled. "Thank you, Annie."

"What for?"

"Coming back for me." Swift's smile wobbled.

"You think I was going to let you sink to the bottom of the North Sea when you still owe the team a work night out? You're not getting away with it that easily."

Swift barked out a laugh and grabbed at his stomach with his free arm.

"Broken ribs too," he said, pained. "Forgot about those for a moment."

"Should you even be out of bed?" Annie said, softly now, reaching out her hand and taking Swift's.

"Technically no," he said, winking. He squeezed her hand with his and rested them on the bed, still wrapped together. "I'm waiting on a bed in the ward, they want to admit me for monitoring and surgery on my shoulder and possibly my ankle. So I snuck out to check on you before I go. But what they don't know won't hurt them."

"Might hurt you though," Annie said.

"Might do," Swift agreed, his eyes catching on Annie's and staying there.

The heat that rose in Annie's cheeks was enough to ward away hypothermia in both her and

Swift, but she didn't care. Not anymore. Swift had seen her in worse situations than with a blush on her face. Like hypothermic in her saggy old underwear with hair that resembled a cactus plant in the desert.

"I might be going to meet my dad," Annie said.

"Wow. That's a big decision."

"Mim knows where he is and I need to take this opportunity. I need to find out what happened with my parents, Swift. It's driving me and Mim apart."

Swift stroked at Annie's hand with his thumb, almost absentmindedly. Outside the curtain an alarm went off and a scurry of activity followed. Inside the cubicle the detectives were wrapped in a cocoon of their own making.

"That's very brave of you, Annie. I'm really proud." Swift nodded slowly, his eyes focussed elsewhere. "I hope you get what you need to out of meeting him. And I'm here if you need me too."

"Thanks, Swift, I appreciate that," Annie said, gripping the blanket around her chin as it started to slip. "I appreciate everything you've done for me."

"You sound like you're about to say goodbye, Annie," Swift said, frowning. "Are you about to say goodbye?"

Did she? Was she? Was Annie about to leave the comfort of the MCU and the best friends she'd made there to go and find her father and get to the bottom of the mystery of her parents? That wasn't what she'd meant, but now she was saying it out loud maybe there was a reason Swift had heard an unspoken goodbye.

"Annie," Swift said, quickly, before she could reply. "You're doing something very brave. Something that could upend your life and everything you thought you knew about your parents. I don't want you doing that on your own."

"Neither do we," a voice said from the other side of the curtain.

Annie and Swift looked at each other, eyebrows raised.

"Show yourselves," Annie said, peeling her hand out from under Swift's in case whoever it was got the wrong idea about them.

And the curtain opened once again to reveal the tired faces of Page and Tink.

"If you think you're getting out of the MCU that easily, you need to think again," Tink said, blowing Annie a kiss.

"Funny, I said a similar thing to Swift about our work night out." Annie laughed.

"Honestly, though, Annie," Tink went on. "We're here for you. And we need you too. Our little team has been way more cohesive since you joined us. We work as a quadruple; your brain works in ways ours don't. Candy wouldn't have made it if it wasn't for you. Neither would Benjy."

"How are they?" Annie asked, momentarily forgetting her parents.

"They'll be okay," Tink said. "They're at Candy's,

staying there until something permanent can be sorted for Benjy. Raven is back with her Order family too. All's as well as can be expected."

Annie nodded, relief flooding her that the kids were okay. She caught Swift in the corner of her eye, he was tapping the wheel of his chair with his finger, his brows furrowed.

"Guys, can you give us a minute, please? I was trying to say something to Annie," he said, pushing open the curtain to show them the way. "Page, don't you have a sergeant's exam to prep for? Tink I'm sure you've got notes to be writing."

They shuffled out and the silence descended again. Swift looked pink cheeked.

"Annie what I was trying to say before we were interrupted is that you're being very brave in facing something that might change your life completely." He cleared his throat. "So, I'd like to do the same."

Annie felt her stomach tighten and she held her breath as Swift took her hand back.

"The code to my phone, the date I said changed my life, fourth of August, do you know what it is?"

Annie wracked her brains but ended up shaking her head.

Swift inflated his lungs and winced at the pain.

"It's the first day I met you, the day you walked into the station to talk to me about Tim Barclay in relation to his missing daughter."

Annie felt a sob bubble up in her and Swift continued.

222

"When I'm out of here and back on my feet, I wonder if you'd like to come with me... um... out, you know, on a date?"

There was a whoop of joy from outside the curtain as Tink and Page started clapping. Swift's face turned the colour of his bruises and Annie's matched. She felt like a corner had been turned and Annie realised that the MCU were her family. She didn't need to leave them in order to find out more about herself. There was no need to run away from them because she was facing something difficult. They were there for her just as she'd always be there for them. She turned her attention back to the DI, to Swift, to Joe and found her smile growing.

"I'd love to," she said, leaning over in the bed as far as she dared and giving him a kiss on the cheek. "Just promise me it won't be to a magic show."

Swift laughed and winced and gently grabbed Annie's chin with his only good hand, turning his face towards her. He bent as far as his ribs would let him and, there in the cubicle of A&E surrounded by machines and noise and the listening ears of their colleagues, Swift finally pressed his lips to Annie's and kissed her.

THANK YOU!

Thank you so much for reading VANISHING ACT. It's hard for me to put into words how much I appreciate my readers.

If you enjoyed VANISHING ACT, I would greatly appreciate it if you took the time to review on your favourite platforms.

You can also find me at www.KTGallowaybooks.com

ALSO BY K.T. GALLOWAY

Annie and Joe will be returning in August, you can pre-order their next adventure now!

PRE-ORDER NOW!

The O'Malley & Swift adventures available to buy now!

CORN DOLLS

Their first case sees Annie and Joe on the hunt for a young girl who is missing. Snatched from her home during a game of hide and seek. Left behind in her place is a doll crudely twisted from stalks of corn.

FOXTON GIRLS

When a spate of suicides occur at prestigious girls' school, Foxton's, Psychotherapist Annie O'Malley is called in to talk with the students.

What Annie finds are troubled young girls full of secrets and lies; and a teacher caught in the midst.

WE ALL FALL DOWN

When a young woman falls ill and dies after a night out, her friends blame a cloaked figure that had been stalking them in the streets. A masked face with hooked beak, immediately recognisable as a Plague Doctor.

THE HOUSE OF SECRETS

With a lead on her missing sister, Annie and Joe travel north and rent a small cottage in the village where Mim was last spotted. Only, the village has a dark history of its own. The cottage was home to a family who haven't been seen in over forty years. Their things still packed away in the basement, awaiting their return. It's a macabre destination for the dark tourist, and the rest of the village isn't much more welcoming.

THE UNINVITED GUEST

Back in Norfolk and back to work, Annie O'Malley and DI Swift are called to an isolated seaside village and the exclusive Paradise Grove Spa. Renowned for its peace and tranquility, the spa and its staff offer the chance to relax and recuperate in a discrete private setting on its own causeway. So when a dead body turns up in one of the rooms with no clue to who he is or how he got there, suspicion falls on the secretive group of guests.

DEADLY GAMES

When Annie and Joe are called to the local park to investigate reports of vandalism, they begin one of the most harrowing cases of their career. The vandal is a scared young woman with a bomb strapped to her chest and a list of games she must play. As the games get more gruesome, the young woman has a choice to make; kill or be killed.

ONE LAST BREATH

After the distress of Annie O'Malley's last case, she's in need of a bit of rest and recuperation. So her sister, Mim, books them on a flight to a luxury all inclusive resort in Spain for a break. But what was supposed to be a chance to sip sangria and reconnect with each other after so long apart soon turns into something terrifying when a group of armed men storm the hotel and take the guests hostage.

VANISHING ACT

When the celebrated illusionist, Gabriel Mirage, is found dead in the midst of his own vanishing act, O'Malley and Swift are thrust into a realm where the truth is as elusive as the disappearing act itself.

Printed in Great Britain
by Amazon

43725184R00138